BED-AND-BREAKFAST BLUES

Other Books by Susan Ralph

Brompton Manor
Starting from Scratch

BED-AND-BREAKFAST BLUES

•

Susan Ralph

Text copyright ©2011 by Susan Hamilton
Printed in the United States of America.

Published by Montlake Romance
P.O. Box 400818
Las Vegas, NV 89140

ISBN-13: 9781477813546
ISBN-10: 1477813543

To my husband, who made all my dreams come true

Chapter One

Rain drummed a steady beat on the roof over my head. Songs on an oldies-but-goodies station playing on my kitchen radio supplied the melodies.

I dried the pan I'd used to heat up my dinner and glanced out the window over my kitchen sink. In the far corner of my backyard, rainwater flowed over the rim of a neglected bird-bath.

A good night to stay inside.

Not that I had anywhere to go.

After five years of lackluster men and meaningless dates, I'd grown weary and wary of men. So, I was on sabbatical from dating—a time-out to recharge my spirits and restore my belief that the right man would show up at the right time.

Since starting my yearlong sabbatical six months before, spending my nights at home, even when the weather was good, even when it was Saturday night, had become routine.

It freed up hours of unscheduled time and an abyss of unused emotional space. To fill the void, I'd been reading the books on my "to read" list, and I had adopted a dog from the no-kill shelter. The Earl of Bowser was a regal male cockapoo who stole my heart.

Having a dog rather than a man in my life was an eye-opener. He was eager to learn how to please me. He wasn't afraid to express his love for me. His needs were simple, his demands few. And I could count on him being there for me.

In addition to his other fine attributes, Bowser loves every human he meets. When anyone comes to our door, his tail whips the air like a flag in a stiff breeze. If a stranger leans down and scratches his head or speaks kind words to him, he rewards them with a swipe of his tongue.

He's also better than a broom for cleaning up food dropped on my kitchen floor. But in his eagerness to ensure no morsel of food is left on the floor for more than a second, he keeps his eyes focused on my hands instead of my feet. The third time I came close to tripping over him, I turned off the stove and drove to the local hardware store. I bought two child-safety gates and put them to use that night.

For the first time since he'd moved in with me, Bowser wasn't happy. He stood on the far side of first one gate and then the other eyeing me through the mesh. He whimpered. His eyes drooped. I had to struggle against my empathy for the pain of all living creatures to keep the gates in place.

My safety sense triumphed.

As soon as I finished cooking, and before sitting down to eat, I opened up both gates.

Bowser eyed me with apprehension. I motioned for him to come in. He bounded into the kitchen and went right to work cleaning up the floor.

The next morning, knowing his banishment wasn't permanent, he settled down without complaint and watched through the mesh while I fixed my breakfast.

To reward him for good behavior, I crumbled a crisp slice of bacon and scattered the pieces across the linoleum, then opened both gates.

Tending to my lovable dog and crossing off the titles of the books I'd finished reading gave me a sense of progress and solid accomplishment—a welcome contrast to my long and unproductive search for someone I'd want to marry who also wanted to marry me.

In my sitting room, I switched on the gas fire and picked up my current book, a romantic novel whose virtuous hero made my heart race.

I curled up on the couch and opened the book to where I'd left off. My faithful companion jumped up on the couch, stretched out next to me, and nestled his head in my lap. I rubbed the palm of my hand along his back until it was time to turn the page.

During the first few weeks of my sabbatical, I'd tried to analyze why my methodical search hadn't turned up even one good marriage prospect. At the end of each year, I winnowed down my list of must-haves. A full head of hair and a flat midsection got crossed out early on. But try as I might, I couldn't come up with a good answer to my lack of success. It could be I'd gotten too picky, too quick to find fault. Or maybe the idea of upsetting my cozy world and getting out of my comfort zone made me hesitate to change the status quo. Or maybe the fact that my heart had once been shattered made me overly cautious. Whatever the reason or reasons, there was one requirement on my list I wouldn't cross out. I wouldn't settle for a man who didn't generate more of a thrill than I got when eyeing a platter of Billy Joe's barbecue ribs.

Four months into my sabbatical, I had a startling epiphany.

Even though being in love again would be great, and having a boyfriend or a husband who cared about me would be nice, I was doing okay without a man.

Five months into my sabbatical, I celebrated my twenty-eighth birthday.

Instead of a rowdy celebration at a local club as in past years, I chose to have a quiet dinner at home with Bowser and Marie, my best friend since ninth grade.

Marie showed up with a frosted cupcake and stuck a candle in the top, claiming no one should have a birthday without a cake and at least one candle.

Marie and I were third-grade teachers at the same school in a midsize Southern town where sighting a marriageable adult male was as rare as seeing snow. I'd thought about moving to more fertile hunting grounds, but I loved my house, which got a lot of natural light, and I loved the school where I taught, which had a super student population, and I loved the location, less than two hours from the ocean and an easy day's drive to the mountains. And so my enthusiasm for moving was tempered.

Marie wasn't married either, but she wasn't looking. She was trapped in a ten-year relationship with an on-again, off-again boyfriend. This year she and Jeff had spent more time off than on. Not that I was keeping track on a calendar or anything, but it was now more than a month since she'd heard from him. How much longer she'd hang on was questionable, but she was pretty stubborn. I'd be happy to encourage her to make a final break with Jeff, but she got upset if I said anything negative about him or about their relationship.

With spring break coming up, she and I had signed up for a seven-day Caribbean cruise. In the interval between signing up and the sailing date, we convinced each other a shipboard flirtation wouldn't dishonor Marie's relationship with Jeff or break my sabbatical. We conjured up fanciful scenes of dancing to live music and strolling around the decks with handsome men with foreign accents.

But as soon as we queued up on the cruise check-in line, our fantasy came crashing down. The majority of the passengers in line were families with children ranging in age from toddler to teenager.

We looked at each other and grimaced. Spring break for our school district equaled spring break for untold numbers of others. You'd think we'd have realized these ships would attract families this time of year, but making up fantasies about our cruise had crowded out rational thought. Besides Marie and me, the only people in line with no children looked old enough to have been retired for decades.

Marie and I got our luggage settled in our room, attended the mandatory lifeboat drill, and then sought out the cruise director. He confirmed our sad observation. Marie and I were the only passengers younger than sixty without children.

During the day, noisy splashing youngsters took over the pool area—except for the hour set aside each day for adults-only swim, when the throat-clearing nursing home set took over.

At night, the main dining room and the showroom were turned into scenes of chaos as parents dealt with their energetic offspring. I wanted to create and wear a big sign that reminded these parents that letting monsters eat foods high in sugar was a crime against their fellow passengers. Marie discouraged me, fearing we'd be shunned or, worse, pushed overboard. I tried to avoid noticing the quantity of sugary delights the high-energy persons less than five feet tall devoured each day, but the ill effect from their indulgences couldn't be avoided.

The bars and casino were the two grown-up sanctuaries on the ship. Neither Marie nor I drink anything more potent than lemonade. And neither of us would risk our hard-earned money

Susan Ralph

by inserting coins into the slot of a gaudy, noisy machine or by handing it over to a sharp-eyed human running a gaming table.

During the ship's days at sea, we spent the next month's grocery money on expensive massages, facials, and manicures. When the ship anchored in port, we spent the following month's grocery money on expensive shore excursions. All of these unplanned expenditures got charged to our credit cards. Each time I handed my card to a smiling ship's employee, I grumbled aloud about the extra debt I was running up. Their response was to offer me a knowing look and a wider smile.

Our one free escape from the turbulent energy of the public areas was our room's private balcony—which turned out to be worth every penny of the higher room charge. Each morning after breakfast, we sprawled out in the lounge chairs to read the novels we'd packed along with our cocktail dresses and spike heels. We soaked up the salubrious air of the Caribbean during those quiet interludes. But, after an hour or two, we'd get bored and then venture out to find somewhere to sit and observe scenes resembling recess on a school playground.

To put a positive twist on a negative, we decided as unmarried childless schoolteachers we could use the time to study the interactions between husbands and wives and their offspring. So we bought notebooks and pens and began taking notes. As the various members of a family met and separated, we noted the intricate web of memories and experiences they were weaving around their family unit. Both Marie and I are from broken homes and mindful of how fragile the strands binding a family together can be. We picked out three families, jotted our notes about them, and then discussed our observations over dinner. We'd never know for sure, but we concluded only one of these husbands and wives would not divorce.

The cruise wasn't a total loss. The manicurist had a real talent for her work. My finger- and toenails had never looked better.

And then there were the perks of having one's bed made and one's meals prepared. But the biggest perk for me was being on the ocean. The salt-infused air soothed my soul and helped soften the toxic effect of being captive in a confined space with a large group of elementary-aged children over whom I had no control.

On the third day of the cruise, Marie and I pledged to try to focus only on the positives. We held to our pledge most of the time, but when we disembarked for the last time, our disenchantment with the cruise and our worry over the extra debt we'd accrued left us feeling dejected.

We caught the return flight to the airport closest to our town, picked up my car from the long-term parking lot, and set out for home. I dropped Marie at her apartment and then drove to the boarding kennel to retrieve the Earl of Bowser.

The instant my faithful and loving dog saw me, the switch on his tail flipped to high speed. And—I swear to the truth of this—he grinned at me.

I bent down to say hello. His wet tongue swiped my face. He snuggled against my side. No human male had ever given me so much for so little.

I got Bowser in the car and drove home. The peace and quiet inside my house settled over me like a down comforter. I let Bowser out to inspect his backyard domain while I got my luggage out of the car. After dinner, he and I settled down in front of the television until bedtime.

Adopting Bowser had been my best decision in a long time.

The day after we returned from the cruise was a workday. When I got home from school, my mailbox was stuffed with a week's worth of mail the post office had held while I was gone. I carried the bundle inside to the kitchen.

Standing next to my kitchen table, I separated the junk mail

and the bills into different piles. Near the bottom of the bundle
was a letter-sized envelope with my Aunt Della's return address.
I set it apart.

Out of the corner of my eye, I saw Bowser standing in front
of the sliding glass door that opens to the backyard.

I let him out, and then went to my bedroom and changed
into my pj's.

I headed to the kitchen to start dinner.

"Arf, arf, arf."

Strange. Bowser never barks, not even at squirrels with the
nerve to invade his territory.

"Arf, arf, arf," faster and louder.

I looked through the kitchen window into the yard. I didn't
see Bowser. I opened the back door and stepped out. Bowser
was nowhere to be seen, and the fence gate was partly open.

Not a good sign.

I padded down the hall to the dining room to get a view of
the front yard.

Poised in a defensive stance, Bowser was holding a man at
bay at the edge of my driveway—a man whose physical attributes qualified him for the romantic lead in a movie.

The movie-star man spotted me and waved.

"Hello," he hollered. "Can you call your dog off, please?"

Bowser is a lover, not a fighter. He's never threatened
anyone—which caused me to question the wisdom of calling
him off. Curiosity overruled caution. I opened the front door.

"Bowser, come here."

He remained frozen in place. Only his fierce barking made
him distinguishable from a piece of yard art.

"Lady, I'm just here to deliver a package." The man lifted his
right hand. His fingers were clamped around a small parcel
wrapped in white butcher paper and tied together with string.

"Set it down and walk away," I shouted.

"It's cheese, and it's perishable," he yelled back.

"Are you sure you're at the right address?"

"1503 Dailey Drive?" He glanced at the numbers tacked above my front door.

"Who are you looking for?"

He looked down at the wrapping. "Miss Honey Benton."

My pj's were opaque. The neck was high, the sleeves were long, and the legs came all the way down to my ankles. Pretending I was dressed in street clothes, I ambled across the grass, picked up Bowser, and then carried him inside. I pulled the front door closed until only a slit wide enough to keep the man in sight remained. "Okay, set the package down and then leave." I called in my best schoolmarm voice.

The man didn't obey me any better than Bowser had.

He started up the driveway.

Bowser growled low in his throat.

I used my foot as a wedge to keep the door in position so Bowser couldn't get out.

The man catapulted up the porch steps. And then, standing less than an arm's length away from the door, he held out the package.

"You Miss Benton?"

"I am." Fear or desire made my normal breathing difficult.

He smiled—a smile that could thaw a heart frozen as solid as the ice blocks of an igloo.

"Your Aunt Della said to make sure you get this. I figured I couldn't say you did if I didn't hand it to you."

A bolt of caution shot through me. Had Della really sent him?

"You know my Aunt Della?" My voice squeaked.

"Yup. I do odd jobs for her."

I managed to narrow my eyes and lower my voice. "Like what?"

"Fixing broken stuff. Putting up hurricane shutters. Relighting pilot lights." His guileless eyes, the same green-blue as the Caribbean Sea close to shore, grabbed onto mine and wouldn't let go.

I heard myself gasp for air.

He grinned. His eyes flickered with amusement. "Delivering packages to her niece."

I widened the slit between the door and the frame far enough to get my hand through.

"Tell Della your delivery was a success." His fingers brushed mine as I took the package. Touching a live wire wouldn't have been more electrifying. "And tell her I said thank you and hello."

He gave me a dazzling smile, a quick salute, and then turned on his heel and headed for the Jeep parked at the curb.

I watched his retreat, too mesmerized to do anything but stare. He moved with the athletic grace of a running back weaving through a flurry of defenders. Something inside me melted like a Popsicle on a hot day.

But my dog who loved everyone did not love Mr. Romantic Leading Man. And, even if he looked like he might qualify as a right man, this was the wrong time.

He drove off, which cured the paralysis he'd caused.

I closed the door and then hurried back to the kitchen and snatched up Della's letter. I tore open the envelope and read her short note.

Dear Honey,
I'm sending—by special messenger

—a smiley face drawn in red ink grinned at me—

a sample of my new herbed goat cheese. Give it a try and then let me know if you think it'd be better with more or less herbs or a different combination.

And, by the way, if you're free this summer, I could use your help. Millie is touring Europe during June, July, and August.

Love, Aunt Della

My Aunt Della, my dad's sister, is a change-of-life baby, six years older than I. She married at sixteen and divorced at seventeen and then went back to school. She stayed in school until she'd earned a PhD. She'd taught at a private college for five years. When her mother died, Della quit her job and converted the house she inherited from her mother into a B and B. Three years ago a travel magazine featured her B and B as their cover story. The reviewer gave it five stars. Since then, Della has had few vacancies from April through September. I consider her a role model for women who aspire to independence.

Della also owns a small farm off the island where she raises goats and grows herbs. The goats' milk is turned into artisanal cheese and herbal soap. She sells the cheese to a local restaurant and at a natural-foods grocery. She sells the soap at her B and B.

I opened the package and took a sniff. The cheese smelled yummy. I pinched off a sample. It tasted even better.

I pulled out a chair, sat at the table, and considered Della's request for help. I could spend the summer at home with nothing to look forward to, or I could spend the summer at her B and B, which fronted on the ocean, earning money for light work. The extra money would go a long way toward paying off the excess credit card charges from the cruise.

I felt a paw on my bare foot and looked down. Bowser lay sprawled on the floor beneath the table with his nose tucked between his front legs. He lifted his head and looked at me with a pitiful expression in his eyes.

I slid off the chair and joined him on the floor.

He placed his head in my lap. "It's okay, buddy. I promise

I won't desert you. If Della says you can't come, I won't go." I scratched his head and made cooing sounds. "You know your happiness always comes first."

In the midst of my assuring Bowser there was no reason for him to worry, my thoughts drifted off to my own reason to worry. If I worked for Della this summer, would the cheese-delivery guy be around? And if he were, would—?

Silly me. I never change course midstream unless I run into an obstacle I can't find a way around. And when I set a goal, I don't abandon it until I've accomplished what I set out to do. Unless, after I've done everything I could to succeed, success isn't possible.

My no dating for a year had been going great so far. I had several things I was working on during my time-out. Among them was regaining a levelheaded approach to men, rebalancing my emotions, and erasing a sense of desperation that had begun to control my decisions. A premature end could be folly.

I jumped up and clicked on the television, hoping the sounds and the flickering screen would distract my imagination from its fantasies about Della's handyman.

There were several compelling reasons to work for Della this summer—and her handyman wasn't one of them.

I secured the child gates in the openings to the kitchen and started browning ground beef for spaghetti sauce.

When I'd finished fixing my dinner, I let Bowser into the kitchen. His entire body drooped. He lapped up water from his bowl and then turned and walked out of the kitchen with his tail and his head down. For the first time since I brought him home, he hadn't scoured the floor for food.

Strange.

After dinner, I curled up on the couch and turned on the television. Bowser didn't join me.

The local newscast ended. I switched off the television.

Bowser went to the sliding glass door that opens to the back-yard.

I let him out. Two minutes later he had his nose pressed to the glass. His usual routine on the last trip outside for the night is to spend at least fifteen minutes or more in the backyard. If he didn't perk up by morning, I'd make an appointment for him with the vet.

I got ready for bed. As soon as I snuggled under the covers, Bowser jumped up on the bed, which wasn't allowed unless I invited him.

But he'd shown a sensitivity to my moods before. Maybe he sensed my tension over whether or not to say yes to Della.

I let him stay on the bed.

He made himself comfortable and within seconds he was asleep.

I closed my eyes. Tantalizing scenes of a summer romance at the beach kept me awake. I turned over to my stomach and buried my face in my pillow. Get real, Honey. The romantic notions you and Marie dreamed up about a shipboard flirtation didn't pan out. And the odds of romantic notions you dream up about a summer flirtation at the beach panning out aren't much better. You know nothing about Della's handyman. Not his name, not his marital status. He could have a prison record or custody of a houseful of children.

But what I did know about him made me long to know more. He got an A plus in physical attractiveness and two A pluses for completing his mission despite being threatened by a hostile dog. He had a wicked grin, a pair of eyes one could drown in, and the hint of a sense of humor—even if he'd been laughing at me.

I sat up, turned on my bedside lamp, and then read until well past midnight.

* * *

At school the next day, tired from too little sleep and irritated from dealing with one vexing problem after another, my guard for acting in my best self-interest was down. A summer at the beach would make up for the disappointing cruise and help heal the physical and mental strain caused by months of teaching.

On my lunch break, I called Della.

"Hey, Honey. What's up?"

"If you haven't heard, I got your cheese. I think the amount and combination of herbs is perfect."

"Thanks. Everyone who's tried it likes it. I'm charging a dollar more for the four-ounce package of the herbed cheese."

"Once people taste it, they won't quarrel about paying the extra dollar."

"I'm thinking about expanding my goat herd and increasing my cheese business," Della said.

"Great. I called to tell you if I do work for you this summer, I'll have to bring Bowser."

"So the cheese persuaded you to say yes," she said, followed by her booming laugh.

My protective guard went up again as an image of Della's handyman flitted in front of my eyes. Best to go slow. "I'm not saying I will yet. There are things I have to consider first." I tried for a lighthearted tone of voice. "So who's the cheesecake who delivered it?" A snicker popped out before I could get my lips clamped together. My heart pounded so hard it could have driven an iron spike into a railroad tie.

"Ace Sanford. He's a great guy."

I managed a deeper laugh. "Married?"

"Nope."

"Committed?"

"Nope."

"Is he around the B and B a lot?"

"An hour or so a week."

"Bowser thinks your handyman is dangerous."

"You're joking."

"I'm not joking. When he showed up with your cheese, Bowser forced the backyard gate open and was holding him at bay near the curb."

"Strange."

"Very. He's the first person Bowser didn't love on sight."

"So all this time, sweet, lovable Bowser has been hiding a ferocious guard-dog personality."

I laughed a genuine laugh. "Yup. I was happy to learn a burglar might not get a warm welcome after all."

"I gotta go, Honey. Can you help the weekend of June fifth? It's Cameronfest weekend. I'm booked solid."

"And bring Bowser?"

"Sure."

"Okay. I'll drive down Friday after school. But I'll have to leave Sunday night or early Monday morning. School isn't over until the twelfth."

"Thanks, Honey."

I flipped my cell phone closed. Even if Della's handyman did show up, a weekend of temptation shouldn't be hard to manage. And spending a weekend near the ocean would be a nice break from sitting at home reading. Once I saw how things went during Cameronfest weekend, I'd make my decision about working for Della for the summer.

I jiggled my foot. The same excitement I'd experienced during the first weeks of what had turned into a four-year relationship plucked at my heartstrings. "For pity's sake, you're no longer a naïve eighteen-year-old," I muttered aloud. "Besides you're on time-out. Your man-crossing sign is x-ed over for another six months."

"Pardon?"

I turned to see Mr. Delaney, the school's principal, coming into the teachers' lounge.

"Sorry, Mr. Delaney. Talking to myself."

"Wishing you could be eighteen again?" he asked with a smile on his face.

I sat up straighter in my chair. "Reminding myself how vulnerable and how delusional I was at eighteen."

Mr. Delaney headed for the coffeepot. He ripped the lid off a tub of powdered creamer and dumped the contents into a cup. "As a teenager, I didn't have time for delusions," he said. "I went to school, worked the tobacco fields, and prayed with my family for the right amount of rain and the right amount of sun. A good crop of tobacco put food on our table and paid for new school clothes." He sipped his coffee and then added the contents of a packet of sugar and stirred. "You ever work tobacco?"

"I grew up as a pampered city child. Piano, dancing, and singing lessons occupied my time after school. By the time I was ten, I was a veteran of our local theater productions. When I graduated from high school, my mother urged me to go to New York and try out for the Rockettes. My father insisted I attend university first. He thought I should major in math or one of the sciences. But teaching elementary school is all I ever wanted to do."

"And the Biswell students are lucky you followed your own path, Miss Benton."

"Thank you, Mr. Delaney." I stood up and strolled back to my classroom, feeling lucky I'd been hired to teach here. Mr. Delaney was a gem—with a talent for bringing out the best in people. He worked hard and loved his wife and his children. He was three years older than my father, who also worked hard, loved his one child—me—and I'm pretty sure loved his second wife.

What happened to the males of my generation that made so many of them reluctant to commit to marriage and a family? Maybe social scientists could explain. Or maybe the simple explanation was that, like me, they grew up in a family where their parents' marriage made everyone miserable.

During the days after agreeing to help Della during Cameronfest weekend, I stayed close to home, making only small variations in my daily routine. With the end of the school year nearing, I kept focused on getting my students ready for the end-of-year tests. Seeming to understand my need to concentrate, Bowser demanded little from me except having his basic daily needs met, a few love scratches every day, and a few treats to lick off the kitchen floor each night.

I'd told Marie I'd be working for Della at her B and B during Cameronfest and that Della had asked me to work there all summer but I hadn't decided yet. I didn't mention Della's handyman. If I did, Marie would speculate out loud about my motives for agreeing or not agreeing to Della's request.

I love Marie, but at times she can be exasperating.

The night before leaving for Della's, I packed my bag and then gathered up the things Bowser would need for the weekend.

I'd helped Della at the B and B for a week or two in past years. The shared workload wasn't hard. After the guests finished breakfast and we got the kitchen tidied up, we'd divide up the number of guest rooms that needed cleaning. As soon as the laundry was done, except for the occasional small task or two, my work for the day would be finished.

The rest of the day, Della might work in her office or run errands. Sometimes she'd go to the farm. I'd be free to sit on the beach or to ogle the items for sale in the shops full of art and things no one knows they want until they see them.

The coast of the Carolinas has always been my favorite playground. Each summer, until my parents' antagonism toward each other turned into open warfare, they'd rented a cottage at the beach for the entire length of my school break. During those summers, I'd spend hours searching for intact shells, building sandcastles, and daydreaming. If I spotted a pod of dolphins arcing out of the water, I'd imagine myself swimming out to join them. When the summer ended and we returned to town, my anguish over being landlocked wouldn't begin to fade until my excitement over the winter holidays kicked in.

And despite some not-so-happy memories after I became aware of the tension between my parents, I still loved being there.

I looked forward to this weekend. Being near the ocean and spending time with Della would be a nice break from the past six months of boring weekends.

On Friday I rushed home from school and got Bowser and our gear in my car. The drive to Cameron Beach takes around an hour and a half when traffic's light. I'd be there by supper. I tuned the car radio to a station carrying NPR to catch the news. The hardscape of the city soon gave way to fields of soybeans and tobacco and an occasional small town.

The closer I got to the ocean, the more difficult it became to keep my excitement in check. When I spotted the bridge connecting the mainland to the barrier island, I breathed deep and let my spirit soar as high as it wanted to rise. By the time I got to the other side of the bridge, all the tension in my body and all the weariness in my soul had been expunged.

"We're here, Bowser," I said, sounding a lot like a giddy schoolgirl.

I made a right turn on Circle Road.

An image of Mr. Cheesecake impressed itself on the windshield in front of me. My imagination was out of control. I pushed the toggle that sprays windshield cleaner fluid and turns on the wipers. His image blurred. Sabbatical or no sabbatical, if Della's handyman was around the B and B this weekend, ignoring him could be a problem. "Don't surrender before the first shot is fired," I said out loud to stop my thoughts from tumbling into the world of the absurd. "If this man who Bowser considers a danger to you shows up, you will keep a sizable physical distance between the two of you. You will maintain a cool demeanor. Do not gaze at him for longer than a second before averting your eyes. Do not get into a conversation with him. Give a quick hello, and then turn around and walk away."

Nestled in his car carrier on the backseat, Bowser sounded a snort. With my faithful dog along, I didn't have to worry. The cheese-delivery man couldn't get anywhere near me.

Chapter Two

I turned into the driveway of the B and B. Tall rhododendron bushes, with blowsy pink blooms nestling between dark green leaves, lined the far side of the drive and shielded the neighboring property from the traffic at Della's B and B.

I drove around to the side parking area.

When Della turned the place into a B and B, she added a second story to each of the wings attached to the two-story main house. The addition of the second floors gave her four guest suites in each wing. Her office, a guest parlor, a breakfast room, and the kitchen were in the main house on the first floor. The second floor of the main house was reserved for her private living quarters. On the second floor stair landing there was a small sitting area. Down the hall, on the ocean side, were Della's large bedroom and her sitting room. On the street side, there was a fair-sized bedroom that Bowser and I would occupy. All ten bedrooms had their own connecting bathroom.

I cut off the engine and got out of the car.

In the distance, the sound of the ocean's rhythmic assault

against the shore created a serene atmosphere. A bird flew from a tree to the porch roof.

I opened the door of Bowser's carrier and let him out.

No sounds of human activity could be heard as I carried our things from the car to the porch.

Bowser relieved himself and then joined me. He followed me into the parlor. Della's office door was closed. Knowing health department rules forbade nonhuman animals to be in the kitchen and dining area of a B and B, I carried Bowser up the stairs, settled him in our room, and then went back down to the first floor.

The parlor and the breakfast room had an empty silence. I found Della in the kitchen talking on the phone. She smiled and waggled her fingers at me. I waggled mine back, retraced my route to retrieve Bowser, and then took him around to the beach.

Bowser stayed below as I climbed the steps up to the deck.

Two lounge chairs faced the ocean. I chose one, stretched out, and took in a deep breath. Salt crystals softened and scented the air. I gazed at the scene beyond the deck. Sunlight gilded the tips of the waves. Gulls wheeled overhead. Maybe I'd work here during the summer after all. It wasn't as if I were weak-willed. Life is full of temptations—like hot fudge sundaes—that I resist most of the time.

I adjusted the back of the lounge chair to full recline and then drifted off into a contented doze.

The swish of the sliding glass door woke me.

"Hey, Honey." Dressed in a navy T-shirt and white shorts, Della crossed the deck to the rail. She turned to face me and then leaned back against the railing. "Glad to see you got here safe and sound."

"Thanks. Me too." I sat up and readjusted the back of my chair.

"Where's Bowser?"

"Playing in the sand."

Bowser stopped whatever he'd been doing and bounded up the steps to the deck with his tail flying from side to side.

Della bent down to scratch his head. "Hey, Bowser, glad to see you got here safe and sound too. Mind your manners, and I'll let you hang around the parlor if none of the guests are allergic to dogs."

Bowser slowed the speed of his tail to a steady back and forth as if assuring Della he agreed to her terms.

I joined her at the railing. She gave me a hug. I hugged back.

"If I mind my manners, what do I get?"

Della closed her eyes for a second. When she opened them, she looked into mine as if searching for the answer I wanted.

She turned around to face the ocean. "Make a silent wish for what you want, Honey. I can't guarantee you more than what you have."

Great. So what did I want to wish for?

Wishing for insight into the wisdom of wishing for things in the first place might be a good place to start. No wish is made with strings attached. But a wish come true is likely to come with bungee cords. If I wished for the man of my dreams to show up at the end of my sabbatical and he did, I hoped I'd be ready by then to deal with whatever bungee cords he might come with. At the moment, I was still building up confidence.

"Come on inside," Della said.

"If it's okay, I'll let Bowser stay on the deck for a while."

"Sure." Della stooped down and gave Bowser a pat. "Enjoy yourself out here, Bowser."

I secured the gate so he couldn't get back down the stairs.

Della linked her arm through mine as we went inside and headed in the direction of her office.

Seated at her desk, she pointed to the open page of her reservation book. "The five rooms scheduled to arrive today have checked in. The guests for the other three rooms are due to arrive before breakfast tomorrow. We'll have a total of fourteen at breakfast on Saturday and Sunday."

"Super. What can I do first?"

"We're all set for today. There shouldn't be anything for you to do until morning." Della leaned back in her desk chair and then swiveled around to look at me. "As a sponsor of Cameronfest, I have two free tickets for tonight's barbecue competition. If you want, we can go and sample the entries, and then decide which team to get a plate from for our supper."

"I'd love to. I'll feed Bowser, wash up, and then be ready to go when you are."

Della clicked on her e-mail. "I'll wait for you here," she said, chuckling over something she was reading.

I got Bowser inside the house by way of the street side door and took him upstairs. I'd have liked to take him with us, but I couldn't predict how he'd behave with so much cooking going on.

When he figured out I'd be leaving him, his eyes pleaded with me.

"Sorry, buddy, but your job tonight is to stand guard."

Looking forlorn, he curled up in his dog bed.

Tomorrow, if he was allowed in the parlor, I'd set up the child gate I'd brought from home to prevent him from getting into the breakfast room and the kitchen. He wouldn't be so unhappy when I left him if he could be downstairs ready to greet anyone who came in.

I filled his food and water bowls and then changed into a purple cotton skirt, tank top, and a pair of leather-soled sandals.

I caught my hair in a ponytail, gave Bowser a head scratch, and went down the stairs.

Della and I strolled along the side of the road toward the area where huge lights radiated a shimmering glow. We turned onto a gravel lane fronting the teams' booths. Speakers attached to the top of tall poles wafted beach music through the area. I knew, from having attended before, that the crowd would be huge.

My mouth watered as I took in the scent of burning wood and roasting pork. Colorful banners and flags decorating the booths swayed in the light breeze. Each of the competing teams would be judged on the decoration of its booth, its pulled pork, its sauce, and the required two side items.

Della and I made our way along the row of booths, stopping at each one to sample their barbecue and offer compliments on their decoration.

"This year," Della said as she licked sauce off her fingers, "the rules require each team to enter a fried pie in addition to their barbecue and two side dishes."

"Good ol' artery-clogging victuals," I said and laughed. "How people in these parts survive beyond the age of fifty should be of interest to the medical profession."

"You know very well people born and bred here are genetically immune to any bad results from large amounts of saturated fat in their diet. Strangers to these parts are another matter." She boomed out a laugh. "I should put up a sign in each guest room to warn them to watch out for the pork fat."

I swallowed my latest sample. "Maybe the slower pace of life here compensates for the fact that everything is made with or cooked in animal fat."

"Both, most of the time." Della chuckled and waved to the people in the last booth. "The Cameron Porkers, Jaybelle Hayworth's team," she said.

We sampled the Porkers' barbecue. Della looked at me with raised eyebrows.

"The best," was my response.

She turned in her tickets for two plates of the Porkers' pulled pork, beans, and coleslaw, and then carried them over to one of the picnic tables to eat.

I forked up a large portion of the shredded pork.

"Hey, Harry," Della said, as the man she calls her insignificant other scooted in beside her.

"Della. Honey." He nodded to each of us, then plucked a hush puppy off Della's plate and tossed it into his mouth.

"I thought you were fishing," Della said, handing him a second hush puppy.

Harry chewed and swallowed and then picked up the last hush puppy on her plate.

"Was. Nothing biting."

Della shoved her plate across to Harry, set her elbows on the table and turned to me. "They've closed Main Street for shag dancing. There's a live band. Shall we go?"

Nothing in the world, with the exception of the ocean, speaks to me like beach music and Carolina shag dancing. A lot of good memories get churned up when I hear the familiar songs.

During my first two years of college, my friends and I would escape from the campus almost every weekend and cram ourselves into someone's family beach house. In between a few hours of sleep, we'd play cards and shag dance until late on Sunday. My last two years of college, when I'd been in love with the man I thought I'd marry, he and I had competed in shag dance competitions. Most weekends, after I'd started teaching and before breaking up with the committed noncommitter, he and I had spent the weekends either competing or dancing at shag dance clubs at North Myrtle Beach. My ex and I had even won a couple of local contests. But when I gave up on him, I gave

up on shag dancing. My love for him and my love of shag dancing had become so intertwined I couldn't dance without him.

Della invited Harry to join us. He begged off, saying he
had to get up before dawn. He picked up the now empty paper
plate and then leaned over and gave Della a quick kiss. "Y'all
have a good time at the dance." He winked at me, got up from
the table, and said good night.

Della and I headed in the direction of Main Street.

"Two left feet," Della said.

"What?"

"Harry has two left feet. He can't dance. Good at catching
fish though."

"You and Harry ever talk about getting married?" I asked.

"Once . . . sort of. We were crabbing. Harry was hauling in
a crab pot and, without taking his eyes off the pot, he said,
'Maybe you and me should get hitched.'"

"And you said?"

"'You talking to me or one of those crabs?'"

"*Della.*" I sounded just like my mother when she's appalled
by something I've said or done.

Della shrugged. "The subject hasn't come up since."

"Don't you want to get married again?"

"I like being my own boss."

Having no idea how being married changed a relationship,
or how it interfered with being one's own boss, I had no idea if
marriage would be a good fit for me. I'd like to find out though,
give it a try—see if being legally bound to someone agreed with
me. But, the truth was, I was conflicted. The institution of marriage hadn't worked out so well for my parents, or for a lot of
my friends' parents, or for Della. But when I read the anniversary celebration announcements on the social pages of the Sunday newspaper and saw the photos of the couples celebrating
twenty-five, or fifty, or every now and then sixty years of mar-

riage, my lack of faith was proven wrong. They all looked so happy in the photos. I didn't think they'd go to the trouble of announcing the longevity of their union and include a smiling picture of the two of them if they weren't happy. Therefore, I had to believe, if marriage could make some people happy, it could make me happy too. But if I never found someone special, I'd never find out.

Della and I turned onto Main Street. The short commercial section was blocked off and a stage set up. On either side of the street, rows of colorful paper lanterns strung between the light poles swayed above our heads. People kept filtering in until the blocked-off area contained a good-sized crowd.

I followed Della through the people milling around as she headed closer to the stage. Minutes later, a well-fed, bald-headed man mounted the stage and tapped the microphone. The taps bellowed through the speakers. He leaned his face close to the end of the mic.

"Ladies and gentlemen, on behalf of this year's Cameronfest committee, I welcome you to the twelfth annual Cameronfest Shag Dance Contest."

The crowd broke into raucous cheers.

The announcer motioned for them to quiet down and then leaned in again. "If the contestants for tonight's contest will take the dance floor, we can get started."

A band filed onto the stage. Several couples, with numbered placards attached to their shirt backs, made their way to the open area in front of the stage where a wood dance floor had been set up.

"You shag, darlin'?"

The speaker was behind me and to my left.

I turned my head.

And sank into the sea-green depths of Mr. Cheesecake's languorous eyes.

He held up a numbered placard and then formed his lips into an enticing smile.

"Are you talking to me?" My lips quivered.

"Hm."

An elbow rammed into my ribs. "Honey's a champion shag dancer, Ace," Della said. "You'll be hard put to keep up with her."

Della stepped around me, took the placard from Ace's hand, pinned it to the back of my shirt, and then gave me a shove forward.

Why did I think this had been planned?

Ace grabbed my hand and tugged me toward the dance floor. To my chagrin, I didn't pull back or even make a tiny sound of protest. My power to resist had been mugged by a combination of salt-charged air, filtered light, gentle music, and a pair of sea-green eyes.

The warning to myself about keeping my distance—which I'd reinforced by speaking the words out loud—had been ignored the first time it had been put to the test.

I shook it off. No point waving the white flag of surrender so soon. One dance wouldn't hurt. And afterward, I could re-affirm my rules.

Ace turned to show the announcer our number.

"Contestants number eight. That should do it," the announcer shouted into the mic.

Ace turned to face me. He narrowed his eyes, which served to ratchet up the swelling wave of enchantment rolling over me.

"How's your dog?"

I dried the palms of my hands on my skirt. "Fine. He's guarding the B and B tonight."

Ace placed one hand on my back. His other hand took mine in a loose hold, putting us into the start position.

"Threatening the guests?" he asked.

"Bowser loves everyone."

Except for this man, who was standing so close to me my composure was unraveling. The quivering of my nerves increased until they began pinging a high C. I'd never been nervous when I'd competed in shag dance contests before. Tonight my knees trembled. I struggled to take in sufficient oxygen to keep my head from spinning. The fact I'd never danced with this man before, added to the fact I'd just exposed myself as a wimp, plus the fact Bowser didn't like him, put me on the edge of collapse.

The band struck up the first notes of "Save the Last Dance for Me." And then Ace and I were into the dance and everything worked. Ace not only walked with the grace of a running back, but he also shagged with the smooth glide of an Olympic ice skater. We flowed through the basic steps as if we'd been dancing together for years. My heart throbbed to the beat of the music. By the time the dance ended, I'd entered into a world where a soft glow surrounded every object—including Ace.

"Not bad," Ace said as he made a quick inventory of the outer me.

His look made it unclear whether he was talking about my dancing or about my physical appearance. Whichever it was, his unshielded and brash assessment of me had turned the soft light surrounding him into the harsh exposure of a spotlight. I put Ace into the category of men labeled players—men who charm the most cautious of women into falling in love with them, and then after they hook one, toss her back like a fish who didn't measure up, bait their hook, and recast their line.

I blinked myself back to reality. Regardless of Ace's high marks for his movie-star looks, his prowess on the dance floor, his mesmerizing sea-green eyes, and his one-sided lazy smile which made we want to kiss him, the fact that he was arrogant and cocky had lowered his score to unacceptable.

Digging deep to avoid exposing the strong physical attraction

I had to him, but at the same time not wanting to appear passive or cowed by his appraisal of me, I made a quick scan of him from head to toe. And then I looked him straight in the eye. "You're not too bad yourself," I said without offering even a tiny smile.

"Fair enough," he laughed.

So maybe he wasn't arrogant. But cocky was enough of a character flaw to put him on my loser list.

The judges whispered to one another and then handed the announcer a card.

He tapped the hot mic several times. "Our finalists tonight are contestants five, seven, and eight," he bellowed into the mic.

The crowd broke into loud applause and shrill whistles.

"Finalists, please take the floor for the dance-off."

Ace gave my hand a quick squeeze as we got into position. I recognized the opening notes of "When the Sun Goes Down," one of my favorites. Within seconds, I was caught up in the music and in the coordinated movement of our bodies. It all seemed so right—at least for this moment in time.

And then the music stopped.

Ace slipped his arm around my waist and gave my cheek a quick kiss.

The warm night made me warmer.

I extricated myself from his grasp and then stepped sideways, widening the distance between us to cool down while we waited for the judges' decision.

The announcer repeated his mic tapping. The man had to be hard of hearing.

"Testing, one, two, three!" he shouted. "Can everyone hear me?"

"Yes!" the crowd roared back.

"Good. Before I announce the judges' decision for the winner of tonight's competition, the Cameronfest committee would like me to thank all the contestants and invite them to enter again next year. Now, if this year's finalists will join me onstage, I'll go ahead."

I followed Ace up the short set of stairs. The six of us formed a line to the right of the announcer, who raised his hand and looked at the card he was holding.

"In third place—couple number five."

The crowd whistled, cheered, and clapped as couple five stepped forward to receive trophies.

"Second place goes to couple number seven." The noise of the crowd grew louder.

We'd won. My heartbeat shifted into overdrive. I felt faint. I took a deep breath. This near stranger, this man my dog considered dangerous, had partnered me to first place in the Cameronfest shag dance competition. Being caught in a riptide, with the shore fast fading from view, couldn't have been more frightening.

Ace grabbed me around the waist and then lifted me off my feet.

Dear Bowser, you're right. This man is dangerous. But I'm not totally defenseless. If I keep my guard up, I can resist his alarming magnetism.

Ace set me down. "I've tried to win this contest for four years. When Della told me you'd been shag dancing since you had braces on your teeth, I figured you could be my lucky charm, and I was right." His laugh wrapped around my heart and squeezed the air out of my lungs. "All I had to do was figure out how to get you to dance with me," he said.

Had Della told Ace I was on sabbatical? I narrowed my eyes and directed my gaze to a safe spot over his shoulder. "And 'You shag, darlin'?' was the smoothest line you could come up with?"

The corners of Ace's mouth quirked upward. "Yup. Worked too."

His smile was provocative, straining my ability to remain cool. Something inside me had been released from the prison that had kept it in check. I longed to grab Ace, circle my arms around his neck, and kiss him for real. Instead, I forced myself to take two steps back. My intention to keep a wide physical distance between us and to maintain an icy demeanor had been breached once already. Della would have to find someone else to help her this summer. Seeing Ace on a regular basis would put my sabbatical and my heart in grave peril.

Ace let go of my hand. The announcer handed each of us a small trophy and a check for fifty dollars. We followed the other couples off the stage. At the bottom of the stairs, people in the crowd high-fived and elbowed Ace and congratulated me. After several minutes, I got myself free and found Della, who beamed at me like a proud mother whose child just stole the show.

The minute she and I were alone, my frozen smile dissolved into a frown. Ace, with his beautiful eyes and his skill on the dance floor, would be a great memory one day. But for this weekend, I had to reinforce my defenses and then hold the line.

"What an insufferable jerk," I said in an attempt to convince Della and myself I didn't like the man who'd sent me reeling back into shag-dance nirvana.

"Ace or the deaf announcer?" Della asked and boomed a laugh.

"Is Ace his real name?"

"It's what everyone calls him."

"Can we head back to the B and B? I'm about to pass out from the heat."

"You do look flushed." Della said, adding another of her booming laughs. She threaded her arm through the crook of my elbow. "I knew the two of you could win. Ace took second or third the last three years. He needed a better partner to win."

Had he dropped his old partner because she wasn't good enough? "What happened to her?" I asked.

"She got married and left town a couple of months ago. He's been looking for a new partner but couldn't find one he thought would be a good match who didn't already have a partner. I mentioned you to him." She turned her head to look at me. "You didn't let me down, Honey. You made Ace a winner tonight."

And I'd made myself vulnerable.

We walked along the edge of the road toward the B and B. I was having trouble forming a coherent thought. But Della was on a roll. My silence went unnoticed.

"You're a great shag dancer, Honey. For some reason, you hide your talents."

What talents did Della think I hid? And why would I? When I started teaching, advancing my job skills became my priority. A lot of other things got set aside while I focused on my work. Striving to become the best teacher I could be took up most of my time and energy. And during my first two years on the job, my disintegrating relationship with the man I'd planned on marrying had kept me teetering on the emotional edge of personal disaster. Still, if a friend asked, I'd sing at their wedding. And every now and then I filled in on keyboard for a local jazz group. I'd plead guilty to having given up shag dancing, but my partner had deserted me—and shattered my heart at the same time.

I winced.

A piece of gravel from the side of the asphalt had caught in my sandal. I stopped to work it out so it wouldn't jab my toe each time I took a step forward.

"What are you planning to do with the prize money?" Della asked.

"Buy classroom supplies."

"If I ask her, Serena will highlight and cut your hair for fifty dollars."

"Thanks, I like my hair the way it is. It's easy."

"Okay, a new bikini then."

"I bought a new one-piece last year."

"*Honey.*" Now Della sounded like my mother when she was appalled at something I'd said or done.

We turned onto the long drive leading up to the B and B.

Della stopped me and turned me around to face her. "Stop refusing to spend money to bring out your assets."

I closed one eye. "Fifty dollars in the bank is an asset."

Della pursed her lips together and rolled her eyes.

We kept our own counsel as we went up the drive toward the house. As we got closer, I could see two people sitting in rockers on the porch. We started up the steps.

"Congratulations," they called. "You deserved to win."

"Thanks. It was fun."

"Clay and Donna Bradshaw," Della said. "My niece, Honey Benton. She'll be working here this summer."

I didn't want to contradict Della in front of strangers, but I hadn't said I'd be working here this summer. And after what had just happened on the dance floor, I didn't think I could.

"Lucky you," Clay said. "Grand night." He reached over and took Donna's hand. "The ocean's draped its soft cloak of enchantment over these parts tonight." He turned to look at Donna. She smiled and then lowered her gaze to her lap.

"It has," I replied as a sudden burst of pleasure rippled through me.

Della laughed her booming laugh. "Anyone who works for me has to work from dawn till midnight seven days a week. The ocean's enchantment lures the unsuspecting." Della ended up with her sparkly laugh that makes everyone within hearing laugh too. "'Night. See you in the morning," she said to the Bradshaws.

I formed my expression into an exaggerated grimace, then laughed and said good night. I followed Della inside and up the stairs to the private living quarters.

Bowser greeted us with his usual enthusiasm. I bent down to pet him. He sniffed my hands, my arms, and my chest. He backed away and growled. "It's okay." I said. "I wasn't in any danger. We danced. There was a crowd watching us. And Della was nearby the entire time."

Holding his head high and his tail stiff, Bowser turned and walked back into our room.

"What's wrong with Bowser?" Della asked as she unbuttoned the top button of her blouse.

"He smells Ace."

"Jealous?"

"Suspicious. Did you check Ace's background before you hired him?"

"Ace grew up in these parts, Honey. Everyone around here knows him"—she eyed me with disbelief—"and likes him."

I crossed my arms over my chest. "Bowser has keen instincts about people."

"Competition," Della said. "Bowser doesn't want competition."

"Ace? Not in a million years."

Della boomed another laugh. "The moon is overhead every night, even when you can't see it."

At the moment, Della's over-the-top mood wasn't sitting well with mine. The idea that Bowser considered Ace competition was disconcerting.

"I'm taking Bowser outside, and then a shower and bed," I said with a sound of doom in my voice.

Della appeared not to notice. "See you in the morning. Six o'clock," she said, sounding cheery. She headed for her room, whistling an upbeat tune.

Bowser had no need to worry. Ace had disqualifying traits. To relieve Bowser of any misplaced anxiety, I'd give him lots of attention and assure him of my devotion.

Bowser looked up at me as if trying to discern my thoughts. I reached down and gave him a few head scratches. "Come along, my brave earl, and do not fear, never shall I desert thee for another."

He stayed at my heels as we went down the back stairway and then along a short hallway to a rear door that opened onto the beach. I let him out. When he'd finished, he sped ahead of me as we went back up the stairs. I took a quick shower to get rid of Ace's scent, set my alarm, and then tucked myself into bed.

But sleep wasn't happening. Shag dance tunes kept playing in my head. And so did an undeniable fact: Ace was the perfect shag dance partner for me.

I sighed, turned over, and closed my eyes. Tonight, having been bathed in the sensuous and sultry beach air while dancing to the sweet notes of familiar songs, I'd been spun back into the magical world I'd once inhabited.

Chapter Three

I was still half asleep when I joined Della in the kitchen to help her with breakfast.

Bacon sizzled in a skillet. "Morning, Honey," she said. "Can you crack a dozen eggs and separate the yolks and the whites?"

"Be happy to," I said. I got a carton of eggs from the refrigerator and went to work.

"You sleep okay?" Della asked.

"Hm."

"Last night was pretty exciting," she said, turning to look at me.

"After teaching all day, and then driving here, and then dancing for the first time in years, I was so tired it was hard to get to sleep."

"After we get the rooms cleaned, you can take a nap." Della picked up the bowl of whites and began beating them.

"I may, if you don't have anything more for me to do."

* * *

As soon as the guests finished breakfast and the kitchen was back in order, Della and I gathered the supplies and fresh linens needed to clean the guest rooms.

The guests in my four rooms were tidy. It didn't take me long to clean the rooms and make the beds. I dusted off the tables in the upstairs and downstairs halls, ran the dust mop around the wood floors, and then gathered up the dirty linens and headed back to the kitchen. I stowed the cleaning supplies in the adjoining utility room and then put the used linens in the bin next to the washing machine.

Della was sitting at the kitchen table. "You're fast," I called.

"Lots of practice," she said.

I poured myself a cup of coffee.

A stack of Cameronfest flyers sat on the counter near the coffeepot. I picked one up and joined Della at the table. She was writing up a grocery list.

I studied a flyer that listed the performers and the times they'd be onstage. A fireworks show would end the evening.

"I see a lot of the same performers are back this year."

"Yup. Cameronfest is like a family reunion for some of them. They come back every year to play and to catch up." Della drained her coffee cup and pushed back her chair. "See you later, Honey. There's paperwork waiting for me in my office."

"You want me to go to the grocery store?"

"Thanks, I'll go later. I need to talk to Hal."

Burt's is the only grocery store on the island. When I was young and staying with my grandmother on the island, Burt Delman, the owner and the sweetest man in the world, would let me charge all the ice cream treats I wanted until the end of each week when I'd get my allowance.

"Who's Hal?"

"The person Burt sold the store to. These days, Burt spends his time fishing or crabbing in season."

"I'll miss seeing Burt's big smile."

"Everyone misses Burt, but Hal's doing a great job," Della said.

"I'm going to take Bowser to the beach before I take a nap."

"You and Bowser enjoy," Della said. "It's a beautiful day."

Bowser bounded ahead of me and headed for the water. A light breeze cooled the heat of the sun. Breaking waves sculpted scallop-shaped patterns in the sand, and then retreated, leaving behind a trail of foam marking their forward progress.

At the edge of the water, I turned and headed up the beach. Bowser darted ahead. He stopped to investigate something.

I walked past him.

He ran to catch up. He stayed at my side for a few steps and then darted ahead again. The sand and surf, as a substitute for the grass and dirt of his backyard earldom, seemed to agree with him

I moved to where my feet sank into dry sand and then sat with my knees angled up to my chest and watched the waves, the shorebirds, and the people nearby who'd planted umbrellas and set up beach chairs to stake a claim to a section of the shoreline.

When Bowser and I returned to the B and B, I no longer felt sleepy. I got him settled in our bedroom and went downstairs.

I found Della in the kitchen fixing sandwiches.

"Hi, Honey. The celery stalks on the cutting board need dicing. I've got ten tuna sandwiches to fix."

Della offers boxed picnic-style suppers to her guests who put in an advance order.

Twenty slices of her homemade whole-grain bread had been laid out on a long sheet of waxed paper. She began slathering butter on the top of each slice.

I lined up the celery stalks and began cutting them into quarter-moon shapes.

Della topped each buttered bread slice with a dark green romaine leaf.

"Are you going to the grove for the music tonight?" I asked as I wielded a knife resembling a sailor's broad-bladed cutlass across the sliced celery stalks.

Della opened a large can of tuna. "Yup. You?"

I scraped the tiny pieces of celery into a mixing bowl.

Della emptied three cans of tuna fish on top of the celery. Should I risk seeing Ace again before I'd had time to deal with my conflicting emotions about him? Or should I cower in my room and risk nothing? My heart quaked with anticipation or dread, I couldn't tell which. After years of dating men who didn't inspire me, if I lost my nerve the first time I met one who made me tingle all over, by the end of my sabbatical nothing would have changed.

I kicked my courage back into gear. "Sure."

Della got the picnic orders packed, tagged, and stashed in the refrigerator.

She dumped out the rest of the coffee in the pot and then set out a basket of instant coffee and tea. I cleaned the coffee-maker while she filled a bowl with fresh fruit and a cookie jar with homemade cookies for her guests.

"Thanks for the help," Della said. "I've got more paperwork to do."

"I'll be on the deck for a while."

"Okay. I'll see you at five thirty for supper," she said.

I stretched out in a lounge chair on the deck and closed my eyes.

"Hey, Honey," a familiar voice said.

My heart jumped into my throat.

I turned my head toward the steps.

Ace stood on the other side of the gate looking about as good as any man gets.

"Sorry to bother you," he said. "Della asked me to replace the deck light covers."

I sat up. "Sure. Go ahead." I stood up. "My break time is up anyway."

He opened the gate. "Where's your dog?"

"Bowser and I had a long walk on the beach. I imagine he's napping."

I grabbed the handle of the sliding glass door and got inside the house before I saw the muscles in Ace's back and arms ripple as he began replacing the covers on the deck lights.

In the safety of my bedroom, I congratulated myself on handling my unexpected encounter with Ace well. I was pretty sure I'd managed to look and sound normal.

If he showed up at the grove tonight, I'd do fine.

At 5:15, I went down to help Della with supper. After we ate, Della filled the dishwasher while I set the tables in the breakfast room for tomorrow.

We both went upstairs to get ready to go to the grove.

A glance in the mirror informed me the sun had turned my nose and forehead a rosy pink. At the moment my skin looked blotchy, but after a couple of weeks here, my face and any other exposed parts of my body would turn a nice shade of tan.

I took a quick shower and then put on my lime green flounced cotton skirt, a tank top, and sandals. I pulled my hair into a ponytail, twisted it, and pinned it into a knot. With no need to add more color to my face, my final adornment was a pair of silver hoop earrings.

Because the fireworks would make loud booms, I couldn't

leave Bowser here alone. I snapped his leash to his collar. "Tonight, you shall be my prince," I said as we went down the stairs.

Della was in the parlor. Her lips were covered with ruby red lipstick. I figured this meant Harry would be joining us.

She picked up a small cooler sitting near the front door.

We went down the driveway and headed for the grove.

The setting sun had painted streaks of purple and orange in the sky. The birds settling in for the night created a serenade of repetitive notes, while the ocean vibrated the air with promises one could spin into dreams.

I shivered even though tonight's breeze was warm.

We turned off the road and entered the grove. Volunteers had set up rows of plastic chairs. Della and I chose a spot and then claimed two of the chairs. She set the small cooler she'd brought on an empty chair next to her.

"For Harry, if he gets here," she said.

I'd been right about the reason for the lipstick.

Only a few chairs remained empty by the time the bluegrass group, the first of the scheduled performers, took the stage.

The banjo player introduced himself and the other members of the band and then began strumming and singing "Old Joe Clark." I love the twangy sound and the clear sentiment of bluegrass music. Their second song of the night was the wistful "Blue Ridge Mountain Blues."

Bowser was standing in the space in front of my chair. He tugged at his leash. I let my hand drift down and patted his head. "I'll let you run later," I said. "Right now we're enjoying the music."

The band launched into "Orange Blossom Special," a tune that showcases the fiddler.

I tapped my foot in time to the music.

From the corner of my eye, I saw someone inching his way past the people seated to Della's right.

Expecting it was Harry, I turned to greet him.

Instead of Harry, Ace picked up the cooler, set it on the ground, and then sat down.

Bowser growled.

"Hey, Della, Honey, Bowser," Ace said.

I picked up Bowser and tried to get him to sit in my lap. He wouldn't. He straddled my legs and then stiffened his body into the posture of a hunting dog pointing a game bird.

"Good to see you again, fella," Ace said, ignoring the fact Bowser was poised to attack him.

The bluegrass group finished and began dismantling their equipment.

"I can't stay," Ace said. "I've got goats to milk in the morning. Harry asked me to tell you he'll be here as soon as he gets a not untangled."

Della sighed. "By the time he gets here, my lipstick will be gone, and I didn't bring extra."

Ace laughed. "You look great with or without lipstick, Della. I doubt Harry notices anyway."

"He would if I had fish lips," Della said.

Ace patted her hand. "He notices other things about you, like your fried chicken."

Della gave another sigh. "Thanks, Ace. Whatever it takes, I guess."

Had Della sounded annoyed or sad? My heartbeat drummed in my ears, making it difficult to discern any subtleties in tone.

Ace stood. "Evening, Miss Honey, Bowser, Della."

"*Earl* Bowser," I said, like a mother insisting her child's credentials be included whenever their name was mentioned.

Ace looked at me and rolled his lips inward. "Bowser's first name is Earl?"

"His title," I said.

Ace smirked—at least I interpreted the quirk of his lips as a smirk—and then he looked at Bowser and gave a quick nod of his head. "Your lordship, I hope to enlist you in the Cameron Resistance Corps. Our cause is heroic."

Any reply I may have wanted to make got garbled in my churning thoughts. But, by taking a risk and leaving my room tonight, I'd learned Ace was a tease and insensitive. Neither of which was a laudable trait.

Ace gave Bowser a quick salute and then started easing his way back to the end of the row.

Della scratched Bowser's head. "Your lordship, indeed."

To avoid staring at Ace as he departed, I closed my eyes. When I felt Bowser relax, I figured it'd be safe to open them again.

"Ace is a really great guy, Honey."

"He's an unmarried goatherd and handyman."

"And a lawyer."

"Ace is a lawyer?"

"Yup. He works part time at other things because he claims after his first week of practice the thrill of drawing up wills and divorce papers was gone. He likes dealing with goats and repairing inanimate objects better."

"So he doesn't practice?"

"He does, but says there isn't enough business around here to keep him busy full time even if he loved it."

"Fine. But that doesn't explain why he's single."

"It isn't my place to explain Ace's personal life."

"Does he like women?"

Harry plopped into the seat Ace had vacated.

"Does who like women? If you're talking about me, I love

'em. And a woman who can fix great fried chicken goes to the head of the line."

Harry must have run into Ace.

Della laughed. "I hate to tell you this, Harry, but I'll no longer be frying chicken. It isn't healthy. You'll have to find something else to admire about me or take up with a cook at the KFC in Somerston."

On this, I sided with Della. Being courted because you could fry chicken was fine if there were a slew of other reasons too.

Harry took Della's hand and raised it to his lips. "You're looking mighty pretty tonight," he said.

Della pointed out the cooler to Harry. "If you're hungry, there's a tuna sandwich in there," she said with an unusual tenderness in her voice.

Without thanking her or expressing surprise, Harry opened the cooler and got the sandwich out. He removed the wrapping and then took a big bite. After all their years together, I suppose Harry took it for granted Della would provide food for him. I decided to add a new column to my checklist of men's disqualifying traits. If a man expected me to feed him, he wouldn't get on my good-candidate-for-marriage list.

Bowser didn't take his eyes off the sandwich while Harry ate. Harry laughed and then gave Bowser the last piece of the sandwich.

We settled down to enjoy the rest of the music.

The performers put on a great show. After the last group finished, all of the musicians gathered on the stage and encouraged the audience to sing along as they played and sang "God Bless the USA."

The last note sounded.

The crowd rose to their feet, showing their appreciation with loud and sustained applause. When the clapping faded, the hiss and whistle of the first fireworks missile could be heard streaking toward the stars.

Boom.

I picked up a trembling Bowser as the twinkling and popping sparks of red, green, and blue drifted back toward Earth.

The fireworks show went on for several minutes and then ended with a flurry of exploding missiles.

I looked over at Della and Harry. "I'm going to walk back to the B and B on the beach so Bowser can run."

"You want us to come along?" Harry asked.

Had Harry asked because he thought I needed protection or because he thought I needed company—or because being alone with Della created a problem for him? I sensed that as sweet as he is, Harry keeps a lot of himself hidden.

"Thanks, Harry. I'll be fine."

I set Bowser down, and then I hurried off before they insisted on joining me.

The dark beach was deserted except for a couple walking near the edge of the water with their arms wrapped around each other. The moon's reflected light, combined with the light from the houses fronting the ocean, provided enough of a glow for me to see where I was going.

Halfway back to the B and B, I sat down on the sand. Bowser sat next to me. I scanned the dark ocean. Far out to sea, a red light blinked. I looked up. The sky was free of clouds. Multitudes of stars vied for my attention. But I didn't pick one to wish on.

The one thing I wanted I couldn't have yet.

Chapter Four

The shriek of my alarm clock jarred me out of a dream in which I'd been rocking in a cradle formed by ocean waves. In the dream, I'd been floating on my back, staring at the sky, and identifying the constellations. But instead of yellow, the stars were all the colors of a rainbow.

I blinked and looked around the room, reorienting myself back to the real world, and remembered I wasn't at home where I could ignore the alarm clock on weekends. I eased out of bed, dressed, and then, followed by Bowser, went downstairs. I let him out the street side door and waited on the porch to keep an eye on him. A mockingbird in a nearby palm tree was performing a concert of songs stolen from other birds.

Bowser bounded up the steps to join me on the porch. I carried him back to our room and filled his bowls and then headed to the kitchen to help with breakfast.

The smell of coffee brewing told me Della was already there and had started working.

I went through the dining area—and then froze in the kitchen doorway. The person putting a pan in the oven wasn't Della. It was Ace. He looked up and smiled as if his being here so early in the day wasn't something I should be surprised by.

Della was nowhere in sight.

"Morning, Honey," Ace said. He straightened and closed the oven door with his knee. "Pecan rolls."

He looked as yummy as the kitchen smelled.

"What are you doing here? Did something need fixing?"

"Yup. The pecan rolls." Amusement flickered in his sea-green eyes.

"Why isn't Della making them?"

"She forgot—"

I huffed. "Della's been making pecan rolls once a week since she turned twelve and her mother declared the time had come for her to take on the task. Unless she's in a deep coma, she wouldn't forget how to make them."

"—that Harry was picking her up at five to go to his family reunion."

"She could have woken me."

"Hmm. She said she knew I'd already be up, and if she woke you early you'd be grouchy and then growl at the guests."

"She said no such thing," I huffed.

His peach-colored knit shirt, pulled taut across his lean, muscled torso, had the same defining effect as a wet suit. A long white chef's apron tied around his waist covered the front of a pair of faded jeans. His feet sported flip-flops. He had great toes. His skin was tanned. His hair was varying shades of gold. He oozed maleness and radiated a sense of being at ease with himself. I forced myself to move and to stop looking at him.

I stood at the counter with my back to him and filled a mug with coffee. I heard eggshells cracking. It was too much to take in so early in the morning.

The room tilted. My tallying of Ace's assets had made me dizzy. I grabbed the edge of the counter, breathing deep, steadying my knees. When I felt stable enough, I picked up the mug of coffee and then stomped across the kitchen to the sliding doors. I went out to the deck. If Ace could make pecan rolls and brew coffee and do whatever he planned on doing with the eggs, he could get the rest of the breakfast together without my help.

My eyelids sprang up.

Ace could cook.

He didn't need a woman to supply him food. My laugh mimicked Della's booming one. The mockingbird wasn't the only creature who could steal sounds.

I sprawled in one of the deck chairs and sipped my coffee. Out here away from the disturbing distraction in the kitchen, I could focus on the battle between my head and my heart. But it wasn't a fair fight. My heart had been under assault since Friday night, and I hadn't had the time to fall back and regroup. An open war with Ace wouldn't be fair either. At the moment, he had a cache of weapons far more powerful than mine.

A long summer of trying to check my desire to experience his real kiss—a shared kiss, a kiss full of passion—could be my undoing. Not that Ace had given any sign he had an interest in me beyond my ability to make him a shag dance champ.

The glare of the sun intensified as it reflected off the surface of the ocean. My eyes watered. I looked at the pale blue sky dotted with spun-sugar clouds and tried to get a handle on my inner turmoil.

I turned my attention to the flurry of gulls, cawing and swooping through the air. The gulls' activity always seemed so random to me, whirling about and landing for no visible purpose, but I supposed they had their reasons.

I heard someone greet Ace.

I shivered in the heat of the morning as I'd shivered on the night of Cameronfest.

I stayed on the deck until my coffee cup had been empty for

a long time. The longing for a refill drove me back into the kitchen. No one was there. I filled my cup, put a smile on my face, and then stepped into the cozy, light-filled breakfast room. Ace was seated at one of the tables with several of the guests. I glanced at the area where Della sets out the food. It looked fine. I said hello and kept going until I got to the safe confines of my bedroom.

Bowser, who'd been curled up in his dog bed, sniffed and growled. "I'm okay, Bowser. The guests are downstairs, and Ace should be leaving soon."

I put the safety gate in the door of my bedroom and then left the door open so Bowser could see out. I read until I heard the throbbing of the dishwasher. I waited for a few more minutes, and then, hearing no other sounds, I figured Ace had gone and I could come out of hiding.

I crept down the stairs, pausing on every third stair tread to listen. I didn't hear anyone.

The breakfast room was in order. The kitchen was immaculate. A plate covered by a glass dome showcased the leftover pecan rolls. I ignored them and gathered up the housekeeping supplies. Cleaning all of the guest rooms on my own would take a while, and I still had the drive home today, because there was no way I'd be staying here tonight.

I cleaned four of the rooms and then took a break. This time I didn't ignore the pecan rolls. They were as good as Della's.

I finished the last of the rooms and started on the laundry.

I pulled the first load of wet sheets from the washer and then stuffed them into the dryer.

"Hi."

Startled by Ace's voice, I spun around to face him.

"I didn't hear Bowser barking, so I thought it'd be okay to come in."

His tall, lean, muscled body filled the doorway. His smile

warmed my heart. I breathed deep and leaned against the washing machine to support myself. "Why are you back?"

"So you can leave. Della didn't want you to think you had to wait around until all the guests had checked out," he said and stared at me in a manner that made my skin prickle. He lowered his hands, crossed his arms over his chest, and then leaned one shoulder against the door frame—a less tense, less formidable, more heat-stoking posture.

I folded my arms across my chest to form a shield and glared at him—the best barriers I could erect at the moment. "Checkout was an hour ago. The guests who are leaving today have cleared out."

"Good. Then you can have lunch with me."

"No, I can't."

"Why not?"

"I need to finish the laundry and then get on the road."

"I'll finish the laundry later. When I left here after breakfast, I went to say hey to Miss Crandell. When I told her you were here, she promised me lunch if I brought you back with me. Hattie's making potato salad."

Miss Crandell must be in her late seventies now. She and my grandmother had been best friends. They'd both been born and raised here and had never moved away. My grandmother died several years ago, but Miss Crandell kept my grandmother's memory alive for me.

"How is she?"

· "Her mind's great. But, except for visits to the doctor, she stays close to home."

I skewed my lips, weighing my desire to honor Miss Crandell's request against my need to stay a considerable distance away from Ace.

The reality was, it wasn't easy for me to refuse Miss Crandell. I'd stayed here with my grandmother, Della's and my dad's mother, during the summer my parents had battled over the details of their divorce. I'd been a gangly, shy preteen of twelve. Many of those afternoons I'd spent sitting and rocking on Miss Crandell's porch while Hattie, Miss Crandell's live-in companion, spoiled me with homemade cookies and fresh-squeezed lemonade and Miss Crandell listened to me talk about my woes. The comfort she and Hattie and my grandmother provided me that summer had given me the strength I needed to deal with the uncertainty in my life.

Ace grinned at me. His plump, kissable lips framed straight white teeth.

I swallowed hard. A caution—resembling a yellow traffic light—flashed in front of my eyes. I should tromp on the brake of my runaway heart and send Miss Crandell my regrets.

Instead, I hit the accelerator.

"Fifteen minutes. I need a shower."

I hurried up the stairs, took a quick shower, and then dressed in the same outfit I'd worn the night of the shag dance contest. Bowser's eyes followed me as I moved about the room. "I'll be back soon, and then we'll leave for home," I said.

He didn't look happy.

Ace was standing in the parlor. He watched me as I came down the stairs. Presenting a confident demeanor when Ace was around was difficult, but I tightened my lips into a smile and kept my chin up.

He gave a low whistle. "You look great."

Stay cool, Honey. Don't let him see how easy it is for him to rattle you. I focused my eyes on his. "Thanks."

He opened the door for me. I managed to get across the threshold without touching him and then kept a fair amount of space between the two of us as we walked toward Miss Crandell's.

I pondered just how difficult being around Ace for the

summer would be. If I suspended my sabbatical and kept myself open for whatever might happen, and then got my heart broken again, there was a possibility I'd never patch it back together.

The price would be steep.

Maybe it'd be worth it.

I couldn't believe what I'd just told myself.

I could make an excuse and turn around, but I didn't.

"You gonna be my dance partner this summer, Honey?" Ace asked, breaking the silence.

"I haven't decided what I'm going to do this summer."

His thumbs were hooked into the pockets of his jeans. He shrugged his shoulders and then turned his head to look at me. Starlike flickers twinkled in his eyes.

Tempting me to make a wish.

"We could enter more competitions. Try for Nationals. Who knows, we might even win."

"All I'm thinking about is saying hello to Miss Crandell and then getting on the road."

"You might wanna stay for lunch. Miss Crandell and Hattie will be disappointed if you don't."

The old saying that the way to a man's heart is through his stomach has a great deal of truth to it. Marie cooked for Jeff. Della's fried chicken drew Harry. The promise of Hattie's potato salad had persuaded Ace to corral me into this visit. I'd never cooked for my ex-boyfriend. I didn't cook at all until he was no longer around. Maybe that was one of the problems. But even though I could cook now, I wasn't about to woo any man who expected me to cook for him.

"If I'd known Miss Crandell wanted to see me, I'd have come to say hello without the promise of Hattie's potato salad," I said, sounding irritable.

Either Ace didn't notice my irritation or he ignored it.

"Ah, but you have to admit no one makes better potato salad than Hattie," he said, continuing to argue his case.

I kicked a stone. It landed in the middle of the road.

I forced a smile. "You win," I said. "No one makes better sugar cookies than Hattie's either."

"Hmm," Ace said.

I changed the direction of the conversation. "Della told me you grew up here."

"Until I was fourteen."

"And then where?"

"Chicago."

"Big difference."

"You ever see Lake Michigan?" he asked.

"When I was ten, I spent a summer with an aunt and uncle at their cottage on Lake Michigan."

"Compared to the Atlantic Ocean, I wasn't impressed," Ace said.

"It's different, but I had fun," I said.

"I didn't." Ace's tone made it obvious his memories of Chicago weren't good.

He didn't seem to want to elaborate, so I didn't push.

"Is there anything besides age keeping Miss Crandell housebound?" I asked.

Ace lifted his shoulders. "Not as far as I know. She's frail, but she gets herself around the house with only a little help from Hattie." He sounded relieved over the change in our conversation. "She still has her book club. Her bridge group is down to four members now. The youngest is seventy-three. They meet on Tuesdays at her house."

His pensive mood seemed to have lightened.

"We should all be so lucky," I said. "Maybe living in a place where the ocean lends its steady rhythm to life is beneficial to one's mental and physical health."

"I'm pretty sure it helps," Ace said. "People who've lived here all their life expect to live into their late eighties and even into their nineties—unless a shark gets 'em first."

I laughed a genuine laugh. Even if I tried hard not to like Ace, I wouldn't succeed. Except for his persistence in getting what he wants, there were only a few disqualifying traits on my list. And even cocky had lost a lot of its potency since I'd first checked it off after his name. Done right, cocky became endearing.

Ace pointed to a house across the street. "Somebody from off island bought that house a month ago. Word is they're planning on converting it into a B and B. They'll be competition for Della."

"They won't be much competition. Della's place fronts the ocean, which gives her a huge advantage."

"True."

"And Della's breakfasts, when she's there, draw raves."

"I drew raves for breakfast today."

"Did you?"

"You should have stuck around."

"I didn't want Bowser to get upset."

"Is it wise to keep a vicious dog in a public place?"

"The Earl of Bowser isn't vicious. He loves everyone. You're the one exception."

"I wonder why?"

"I doubt we'll ever know." I laughed.

There was a new ease between Ace and me as we turned onto the walk leading up to Miss Crandell's house. I could see Miss Crandell watching out the window. She raised her hand and waved. Seeing her sweet face made me happy. I grinned and waved back.

By the time we got to the door, Hattie had it open. "Miss Honey," she said, wrapping me in a hug. "Miss Crandell is tickled to death you've come to visit her."

Hattie took my hand and led me into the living room. Miss Crandell was seated in a wing chair drawn up to the window. She greeted me with a hearty hello and watery eyes. Her lips quivered.

I bent down and kissed her cheek.

"What a beauty you are, child. Every time I see you, I'm reminded of your grandmama when she was young. I wish she could see how much you resemble her. You give off the same radiant joy."

The part about giving off radiant joy threw me for a second. "Thank you. She set a fine example for me to follow."

And she had. Even during difficult times, my grandmother had remained upbeat and optimistic about the present and about the future.

Ace was standing behind me, so silent I couldn't hear him breathe.

Hattie fluttered her hands through the air. "Y'all come sit down at the table." She grasped Miss Crandell's elbow to help her out of the chair. "We don't want the beans to get cold," Hattie chortled. It was hard to remain down in the dumps when Hattie was around. I think my radiating joy had been sparked by Hattie's hug.

Ace stepped forward. "You go along, Hattie. I'll be honored if such a beautiful lady as Miss Crandell will accept my escort to the table."

Sweetness flowed effortlessly across Ace's lips, making the thought of kissing him even more enticing.

I gave myself a mental kick. Keep it real, Honey. Wishing on stars and creating fantasies is fun but foolish.

Miss Crandell batted her eyes at Ace. "If I were Cinderella, both of my glass slippers would be left for such a handsome and princely escort to find," she said.

Miss Crandell could be a tad on the syrupy-charm side too.

I followed them into the dining room. The table had been set with gold-rimmed china dishes, sterling-silver utensils, and heavy crystal glasses. Ace settled Miss Crandell into her chair at the head of the table. She directed Ace to take the chair to her left, and me to the chair opposite him—which put him in my direct line of vision.

When all the bowls and platters had been passed and we'd filled our plates, Miss Crandell began asking me questions about my work. Education had always been her passion. She'd taught at the elementary school on the island for forty years. During my sad summer here, she'd often spoken to me of the joys of her days in the schoolroom. I think her stories had influenced my choice of teaching as a profession—another reason to be grateful to her.

I related a few amusing and loving things this year's crop of third graders had done and said. Miss Crandell's eyes grew bright, her laughter sparkled. I should have come to see her and Hattie yesterday. But I was glad I hadn't skipped this visit today just to avoid being too close to Ace. And I was glad I'd stayed for lunch. Ace had impeccable table manners, which meant I was getting close to running out of reasons to keep him on my loser list—except the biggest reason of all: my fear of being rejected.

Ace finished the food on his plate and then picked up the bowl of potato salad and offered it around. Neither Miss Crandell nor I took a second helping. Ace scooped the rest of the bowl's contents onto his plate and then added another slice of baked ham.

"I love a man who appreciates good food," Miss Crandell said.

Ace laughed. "It's hard to find food as good as this anymore. Everyone's worried about fat."

"Well, Hattie and I never stopped using lard to make our biscuits and piecrusts. I doubt people die from too much fat in their diet before they keel over from too much worry."

I knew my grandmother had used lard for her biscuits and piecrusts. If Della carried on the tradition, she didn't say so. But because of their flaky tenderness, I suspected she did. And I had no doubt my grandmother would still be alive today if a man driving the wrong way hadn't smashed his car into hers.

"I may start using lard," I said, eyeing the texture of the biscuit in my hand.

"You should," Miss Crandell said. "If you do, you're sure to win hearts."

Ace winked at me.

Thank goodness my face was sunburned. I'd hate it if Ace could see he'd made me blush.

Hattie came through the kitchen door, calling out, "Happy Birthday!" and carrying a cake stand topped with a cake covered in chocolate icing. With the large number of candles poking out of the top, it looked like the back of an agitated porcupine.

Hattie sat the cake stand at the empty place across from Miss Crandell and then took four dessert plates and forks from the sideboard and sat down.

For the first time since I'd met him, Ace looked ill at ease. His eyes were focused on the table.

Hattie struck a kitchen match and lighted the candles. When she had all the candles blazing, Miss Crandell picked up her glass of iced tea and raised it to Ace. "Happy birthday, to the fine young man I'm proud to call my nephew."

Ace looked up. His lips had curled into a tight line. He blinked once and then three times in quick succession, and then he picked up his glass and clinked it on the side of Miss Crandell's glass. "Thanks."

Hattie chortled. "Caught you by surprise, didn't we?" she said. "Well now, you go on and make a wish, and then blow out these candles so we can enjoy my fine cake."

With his hands raised in surrender, Ace looked at Miss

Crandell and then at Hattie. "I should have known the two of you were up to something," he said. He gave a laugh that belied the flicker of sadness in his eyes. "It's been a while since someone made me a birthday cake."

He got up from his place, let out a good-natured sigh, and extinguished the candles with one breath.

Hattie began cutting thick slices of the cake.

Miss Crandell chuckled. "When we heard Honey was helping Della this weekend and the two of you had won the shag dance contest, we made plans to get you here on your birthday and to have a visit with Honey too." She shook a finger at Ace. "Hattie had a hard time loosening up that board on the step you came by to fix today." Miss Crandell giggled.

Hattie tossed back her head and laughed. "Sho' did."

Ace smiled despite his obvious discomfort over the birthday cake and candles.

"When two old women put their heads together to conspire, a wise man should be wary." Miss Crandell glanced at me and winked.

I took her wink as an acknowledgment of my gender—a recognition that one day I'd be a member of the society of conspiring old women.

We ate our cake, and then Ace and I made our good-byes and started back to the B and B. My opinion of Ace's character had gone up a notch. If Miss Crandell and Hattie had so much affection for him, maybe Bowser had it wrong.

"Isn't Miss Crandell too old to be your aunt?" I asked.

"My great-aunt. Her sister was my paternal grandmother. She died when I was four. Miss Crandell took over the role of grandmother. I spent a lot of time with her. She taught me to read. Hattie was sixteen when she came to work for her. The two of them were formidable watchdogs. If they heard I'd got into trouble at home or at school, I'd be in double trouble with them."

"Love's a funny thing, isn't it?"

"Yup."

We walked on in silence. In front of the B and B, Ace stopped. "I won't come in until you're gone so Bowser won't get riled up."

"Thanks."

"When you get back, let me know if you're going to partner with me this summer. If not, I'll try to find someone else."

"Okay." The truth is I wanted to say yes right then and there. At this moment, I couldn't think of anything I'd rather do. When Ace was no longer so close that I could see the swell of his lips and the alluring color of his eyes, maybe I could think about my answer with a clear head—weigh the pros and cons—and come to the right decision.

I turned and went through the front door of the B and B. My feet dragged as I climbed the stairs. Bowser barked. "It's me. I'm back," I called.

When I opened the bedroom door, Bowser bolted out, flew down the stairs, and took up a defensive stance in front of the street-side door. I hurried back down the steps and leaned down to pick him up. "He's gone. And we'll be gone soon."

Crooning soft sounds, I carried Bowser back up the stairs and told him to stay. I took my small suitcase and the bag of his supplies to the car. And then, before I went back up for Bowser and his carrier, I went into Della's office and left her a note saying I'd let her know in a couple of days if I'd be working for her this summer.

A few minutes later, Bowser and I were in the car and headed down the driveway.

I passed the line of rhododendron bushes and turned onto Circle Road, wondering if I'd have the courage to come back.

Chapter Five

As I pulled into my driveway, relief flooded through me.

Ace was at least an hour and a half's drive away. He wouldn't be turning up at unexpected moments and sending my heart rate shooting into the danger zone.

I unloaded the car, let Bowser into the backyard, and then phoned Marie to let her know I was back.

"How'd it go?" she asked.

"Great. I won the Cameronfest shag dance contest and got a trophy and fifty dollars."

"With who?" The drop in her voice made it sound like she thought I was joking.

"A guy who works part time for Della."

"Cute? Ugly?"

"Cute."

"Old? Young?"

"Older," I said and laughed.

"How old?"

I'd counted the candles on Ace's cake, but Hattie could have added one to grow on. "Three or four years older than I am, I think."

"You haven't sounded so giddy since Guy Fallon asked you to senior prom."

"And Guy Fallon turned out to be a dud. He couldn't dance, and all he talked about was football."

"But this one can dance."

"There weren't many contestants."

"Did he talk about football?"

"No."

"What did he talk about?"

"He wants me to partner with him this summer and enter more competitions."

"And you said?"

"I'd think about it."

"Say yes, Honey. Even if you aren't crazy about this guy, you'll meet other guys who dance. With the fickle nature of marriage these days, some of them should be single."

"I hadn't considered meeting other men as a bonus for saying yes."

"You should. You've exhausted your chances around here."

"So, how'd your weekend go?" I asked because I cared how her weekend went and because I wanted to change the conversation—something I'd been doing a lot lately.

"Jeff called. He drove down. We went to a movie. I made him a strawberry pie."

Not so good then. I gave an inward groan.

Marie and Jeff started dating our sophomore year in college. Until we graduated, she baked cookies for him every week, and every Sunday she cooked dinner for him and his roommates. After we graduated, she took a teaching job here and Jeff went home—a two-hour drive away—and hadn't asked her to marry him.

Once, when I'd suggested she move on and forget Jeff, she stopped speaking to me for a week.

"How's he doing?"

"Great. He got a promotion at work."

I didn't know what to say. Jeff works at a car dealership his father owns.

"From general salesman to assistant manager of the used-car department."

"Good. I hope he's happy."

"Honey, I know you aren't impressed with Jeff. But he's a sweet guy. His mother's bossy. She's made him wary of females."

A man who hides behind his mother, in my mind, is not marriage material. "And you're way too sweet, Marie."

"Good night, Honey." She cut the connection.

I went to check on Bowser. He appeared happy to be home ruling over his empire again.

And so was I.

The next morning, I parked my car in my usual spot and headed to my classroom. At the end of each school year, my mood swings between sad and happy. I'm sad because my current students are leaving me. I'm happy because when school starts again, the seats in my classroom will be filled with fresh faces presenting new challenges.

At the end of the school day, I went straight home and let Bowser out and filled his food and water bowls. With nothing else to do, I started thinking about what to do with the fifty dollars. My practical side said I should spend this windfall on necessities like gas for my car or for paying off part of the extra debt from the cruise.

A quixotic whim changed my mind, and before it changed again, I called Bowser in.

"Enjoy your dinner, my friend. I won't be gone long."

At the mall, in my favorite department store, I headed for the swimsuit racks.

Unless I need something in a hurry because of an unexpected event, I never pay full price for clothes or shoes. And this was the beginning of swimsuit season. There'd be no markdowns. I overrode all my usual caution. If I didn't lose my nerve because of Ace, I'd be working for Della all summer and sunbathing or swimming every day. Two swimsuits would be practical.

I chose three bikinis and went to try them on.

Despite my sunburned face, the winter pallor of the rest of my body, and the harsh light in the dressing room, I didn't look too bad.

I studied myself from every angle—a flat stomach, okay thighs, a not-too-broad derrière.

I bought the hot-pink one for full price and drove home feeling liberated in too many ways to count.

The next day, I called Della and told her I'd be there for the summer.

On the last teacher workday of the school year, Marie came into my classroom and sat down. She'd moved into my spare bedroom yesterday to house-sit for me while I was gone. Tomorrow morning I'd leave for the island.

"Want to celebrate with dinner out tonight?" she asked.

"Sure."

"If Billy Joe's is okay, meet me there at five thirty. I've got something I have to do first." She grinned and then jumped up. "Call me if you'd rather go somewhere else," she said as she hurried out of my classroom.

Knowing Marie, she'd gone to buy flowers or a jazzy pair of sunglasses or maybe a book as a farewell gift for me.

As soon as I got home, I'd start packing. Get as much done as I could before I had to leave to meet Marie.

I took down the bulletin board with the summer's suggested reading list, checked the cupboards and drawers one last time, and headed for my car.

With my arms full of files and books I hadn't wanted to leave in my classroom, I struggled to get my key in the front door lock.

Bowser started barking. "It's me, Bowser," I called.

I got the door open. "Bowser, hush. It's me."

He whirled around and took off down the hall. I dashed after him. He took up a defensive stance in front of the sliding glass doors that open to the backyard.

I looked out. Ace was sprawled out in one of my patio chairs. I picked up Bowser and opened the glass slider. In between trying to calm Bowser, I shouted at Ace.

"What are you doing in my backyard?"

"Hi, Honey. I brought a treat for Bowser and thought he might be back here. He wasn't. I saw the chairs and figured a chair would be more comfortable than sitting on the grass while I waited for you."

"So you broke the lock on my gate?"

"I'm good at fixing things. I need to talk to you."

"I have a phone."

"No one answered."

"Where's your car?" I asked.

"At the tire shop."

"You have to get out of Bowser's backyard. And when you leave, make sure the gate latch is secure. I'll talk to you out front."

I set Bowser down, got a hot dog out of the refrigerator, and broke it in half. I broke small pieces off one half and dropped them in a trail from the kitchen to the back door. I waited a few seconds, and then broke the other half of the hot dog into several pieces, opened the slider, and tossed them into the yard. Bowser followed the hot dog.

Busy lapping up his treat, he seemed to forget about Ace.

I opened the front door. Ace was sitting on the stoop. He looked even better than I remembered. In the spirit of keeping my distance, I kept the front door open and stayed close to the house. "What is it you have to talk to me about?"

He looked up at me, focusing his eyes on mine. "There's a shag dance competition Saturday night. I'm asking if you'll go with me."

If he weren't so close, if I hadn't gotten ensnared in his gaze, if he'd called instead of coming here, saying no would have been easy.

I gazed at the porch ceiling. I gazed at the cement stoop. I scooted the doormat back in place with the toe of my shoe.

I found reasons of my own for saying yes.

The main one being that I love shag dancing. The second being that Ace was the best partner I'd ever danced with. Being a shag dance partner wasn't dating, so it wouldn't compromise my sabbatical. And if I kept a tight rein on my emotions, I wouldn't compromise myself either.

My gaze returned to Ace, who was now standing. I let it linger on him for a few seconds. My heart did flips. But I managed to keep control of my breathing.

"Where?"

"Millersville."

Millersville was about twenty miles from the island.

"What time?"

"If we leave by five, we'll get there in plenty of time."

"Okay."

The smile on his face was bright enough to light up the

Grand Canyon on a moonless night. "We'll have real competition on Saturday."

He reached into his right front jeans pocket, tugged out a plastic bag, and held it out.

"For Bowser. From Riff's Dog Treat Bakery."

"Thanks."

"It's a bribe."

I took the bag and tried not to smile. "I'll tell him it's from you."

Ace didn't make any move to indicate he was leaving.

Because I'd agreed to partner him on Saturday, did he think I'd invite him in for a drink or something?

I needed to say good-bye—and fast.

"I'll see you on—"

Marie's car turned onto the driveway. She tapped the horn twice, stopped behind my car, and got herself to the front porch in five long steps.

"Hi. Marie Bates," she said, holding out her hand. She was eyeing Ace the way she eyed a mocha-chip-coffee, double-dip ice cream cone before taking a lick. She ran the tip of her tongue across her lips, looked at me, and grinned.

"Ace Sanford," he responded.

"Ace is my new shag dance partner," I said.

Ace shook Marie's hand. "I'd never won a shag dance competition until Honey showed up," he said, looking at Marie, who is petite, and perky, and pretty.

Marie shifted her gaze to Ace and then back to me. "She told me about winning the Cameronfest title. I hope I can be there next year to watch you defend it," she said.

I fought off a scowl. I hadn't packed anything yet. "I thought we were meeting at Billy Joe's at five thirty?" I said, in an attempt to move things along.

Neither Ace nor Marie looked at me.

"I finished up early." Marie grinned and giggled.

What had come over Marie? Looking at Ace can take one's breath away. But if Jeff was the kind of man who appealed to her, Marie likes men who look a bit odd.

Ace glanced at his watch. "My car should be ready by seven thirty. If one of you'll volunteer to drive, I'll buy dinner."

Marie trilled a laugh. "I'll drive."

You'd think, on the last night before I'd be gone for the entire summer, my best friend would want to have dinner with me without a stranger butting in. But Ace always seemed to get what he wanted. If I could figure out how, I'd have an important weapon in my defense arsenal. If it's his looks, I'll work on neutralizing my reaction—somehow. If it's because he's so relaxed, people feel safe giving him what he asks for, I'll find the will to resist. If it's because he asks in a clear and direct way, I'll counter by learning to say no in a clear and direct way.

"Give me a minute to get Bowser settled," I said.

I stepped into the house. Marie trilled another girlish laugh. "When we were in college—"

I slammed the door shut and sped down the hallway to the back door. I called for Bowser to come inside. He obeyed but refused to look at me. Upset over my betrayal of him, I supposed.

"Hey, buddy." I spoke to him using my most soothing tone of voice. He lay down in the middle of the kitchen floor. I knelt down and took one of the treats out of the Riff's Dog Treat Bakery bag. "Ace brought these for you." Bowser's nose twitched. The bag had to carry Ace's scent, but Bowser didn't growl. I stood up and broke off a piece of the round cookie-sized biscuit and tossed it on the floor. Bowser gobbled it down. I broke up the rest of it and then scattered the pieces across the floor. "Ace may not be such a bad guy after all, Bowser. Goats like him."

Bowser ignored me and continued his quest to find every one of the cookie pieces.

When I got back out front, Ace and Marie were engaged in an intense conversation about goats. They paid scant attention to my return.

I felt a little miffed Marie hadn't told me she'd been a member of 4-H, raised goats, and showed them at livestock events before she moved to my town and we became instant friends. I'm sure I'd told her my Aunt Della had goats.

Marie drove. I rode in the front. Ace sprawled in the back, but this seating arrangement didn't end their conversation about goats. I had nothing to add to a conversation about any kind of farm animal. My only experience with them came from perusing their pieces and parts in the meat and dairy cases at the supermarket, and the places I shopped didn't sell goat meat.

Marie and Ace continued talking about goats on our way to Billy Joe's, and then all through dinner they talked goats, with a break now and then to mention a few other things about themselves. Marie mentioned she had won a shag dance competition once, and that her father was a lawyer. The two of them had a lot in common. I pushed the food around my plate and gathered more facts about goats than I'd ever use unless *Jeopardy!* had goats as a category one night—which I doubted would ever happen.

We dropped Ace at the garage where his car was being serviced.

"'Night, Marie. 'Night, Honey. Thanks for helping me out tonight." Ace got out, then leaned down to look at me through the passenger window. "Saturday at five. I'll pick you up."

"Okay," I said, without much enthusiasm. The troubling truth I'd learned tonight was that the thrill I get from seeing a platter of Billy Joe's barbecued ribs pales compared to the thrill I get from looking at Ace.

My heart zoomed around a blind curve.

The road ahead was dark as pitch.

But I hadn't committed to partner Ace beyond Saturday night. On Saturday, I'd concentrate on dancing. Afterward, I could tell him in a clear and direct way I wouldn't partner with him again—if that's what I wanted to say.

The car tires squealed as Marie wheeled her car out of the garage parking lot and got us back on the street.

"Wow," she said, waving her hand over her face like one does when feeling overheated.

Marie had a case of the vapors. I had a sinking feeling in the pit of my stomach.

"Good luck, Honey."

"About what?" I croaked.

"About Ace."

"Except for the fact he's a great dancer, Ace and I don't have much in common. Besides, he has a check mark on every item on my men-to-avoid list."

"Like he's so hot your eyes melt?" Marie laughed.

"Like he thinks goats are interesting. How come you never told me you used to show goats?"

"By the time I met you, I was more interested in talking about boys."

That made sense.

Marie stopped for a red light and turned to look at me. "Guess where I went after school today?"

"I have no idea," I said, expecting her to pull out a gift.

Marie laughed that silly laugh of hers that makes her sound like a munchkin.

"I met Jeff at Biswell Jewelers."

Shocked, I spun my head around to look at her. "You did what?" I shouted.

"We bought my engagement ring."

"You didn't!"

"We did. I didn't say anything to you before we bought it for fear I'd jinx my luck and Jeff would back down."

"I don't think your engagement has anything to do with luck, Marie. You've worked hard at rounding Jeff up."

"Stubborn critter, isn't he?"

We were laughing as Marie turned the car into the driveway. "So where's the ring?" I asked.

"Being sized."

"How come Jeff didn't take you to dinner?"

"He had to get back to work."

"You have to promise me when you get your ring, you'll drive down to the beach and show it to me."

"I promise. I'd like to see Della's goats too."

I was happy because Marie was happy, but not about her marrying Jeff. In a lot of ways, she and Jeff are opposites. She's sweet almost all of the time. He's surly most of the time. She bends over backward to please him; he doesn't bend at all. I doubted they'd be announcing their twenty-fifth wedding anniversary in their local newspaper. But who was I to think I understood anything about love? How many years had it taken me to admit the reality of my relationship with the noncommitter? And then, after I'd seen the light and ended it, how many years had I wasted by avoiding promising men because I feared making a mistake again?

My eyes widened.

A truth I'd never admitted before hit me hard.

If all the men I'd dated since my breakup had been losers, it was because I chose to date only men I knew I'd never fall in love with.

My sad record now made sense.

And now there was Ace, who I thought I was already in love

with. Maybe this summer would be a good time to test my heart.
Find out if, during the six months of my sabbatical, I'd made
some progress toward being willing to put my heart at risk
again. But I was only spinning dreams. Ace hadn't given me a
single reason to think he was interested in having a romantic
relationship with me. In fact, after I gave him what he wanted
by agreeing to partner him on Saturday, he'd pretty much
ignored me.

Chapter Six

As soon as Marie and I came through the door, Bowser, who was waiting for us in the small entrance foyer, got to his feet and began sniffing us. If he did detect Ace's scent, he didn't back away or growl.

Marie said good night and headed to her bedroom.

I went to the kitchen to put my take-home box into the refrigerator and then checked my cell phone.

There was one voice mail. From Della. Her message said the kitchen area of the house the new owners may be turning into a B and B had caught fire. Sheriff Pitts had stopped by to talk to her. He said he was pretty sure it was arson. She suspected she was considered a prime suspect since she'd have a motive. She said she had no witness to verify her whereabouts at the time the fire must have been started.

Not one person who knew Della would believe she'd resort to burning down her competition. She loved challenges. In her early teens, before her premature marriage, she'd competed on the junior tennis circuit. If a new B and B opened, she'd work day and night to best them fair and square, and she'd love every minute.

Since Della went to bed early most nights, I didn't want to call and wake her. Tomorrow I'd be there and could get all the details and offer my support. Seeing her face when I talked to her, I'd be better able to tell how worried she was.

I went to pack.

The hot summer ahead of me just got hotter.

By the time the feeble morning light prodded me to get out of bed, I'd been awake for five minutes or more dealing with my excitement and thinking about the changes working for Della this summer could bring. I'd get my credit card paid off in full. Except for my mortgage, I'd be debt free. I could afford graduate-level classes toward my master's degree.

I staggered to the kitchen and started a pot of coffee. By the time I got Bowser though his morning routine, the coffeepot was full.

Marie shuffled in, wearing a granny nightgown and a pair of bunny slippers. She poured coffee into a mug.

"It's awful early, Honey. What time are you leaving?" she asked.

"Around ten. But I'll be gone from here by eight. Bowser has an appointment with his groomer. As soon as he's bathed, trimmed, and fluffed, we'll head off for the island."

"Okay. I'm going back to bed. The best thing about the end of the school year is taking a full week to do what I want to do, which is nothing."

"And I've agreed to start working for Della this summer without taking a break first." I made a sour face.

Marie laughed. "Right. I don't recall hearing you dither over whether or not you wanted to work there this summer."

"Well, I did. I didn't share my changes of mind with you

because I needed to work through my panic on my own. More than once, I teetered on the brink of not going."

"Della knew what she was doing when she sent Ace to deliver the goat cheese."

"Ace didn't influence my decision. I considered doing a lot of other things this summer. But the extra charges from our cruise put me in a big financial hole, and the idea of a summer by the ocean was hard to resist."

Marie skewed her lips and rolled her eyes. "Right."

"I'm not the starry-eyed girl I once was, Marie."

"Love's a funny thing, Honey."

I raised my eyebrows. But I couldn't claim it wasn't, because if love weren't a funny thing, she wouldn't be marrying Jeff.

I pulled together the bags and boxes of a summer's worth of gear for me and Bowser, got everything in my car, and then settled myself in the driver's seat. Marie stood in the open doorway and waved as Bowser and I drove off.

With Marie house-sitting, I wouldn't have to drive back here once a week to check on things. In fact, my house would benefit from Marie living there. Not only was she three times neater than I, her father had taught her how to do simple home repairs. She could change a faucet washer, replace a ceiling light fixture, and unplug a drain. She understood things like shutoff valves and fuse boxes. Skills she had in common with Ace.

I lack all handyman skills and counted on Marie to take care of those things for me even when she didn't live in my house. My payback for her work had always been a promise to sing at her wedding. But after she married Jeff, she'd move away, and I'd be on my own. Before her wedding day, I'd have her teach me how to do simple home repairs. It would save me a lot of money and would make me more independent.

* * *

While the groomer worked on Bowser, I ran a couple of last-minute errands. At 9:55, I returned to pick up Bowser.

The groomer brought Bowser to the front. "How regal you look, your lordship," I cooed. "The quality of your coat befits an earl of the dog kingdom."

Bowser wagged his tail and licked my hand as I placed him in his carrier for our drive to the beach.

"You understand we're spending the summer at Della's and she expects you to behave," I said as I settled the carrier in the car.

I got no response, but I had no qualms about his behavior while we were there. Aside from his inborn curiosity, which sometimes leads him astray, and his dislike of Ace, Bowser is obedient, well-mannered, and lovable.

As we drove along the near-deserted roads, I wondered if this summer would change my life for the better—if nothing else, get me out of my dreary rut. Della's B and B drew all kinds of people. A couple of times, she'd mentioned that several great-looking single men who sailed had booked a room during spring regatta week. Maybe one or more of them would return this summer.

The closer I got to the island, the more positive my outlook about the summer. I could end up running aground on the rocks, but until I did, I couldn't think of anywhere I'd rather be.

Chapter Seven

As the miles zipped by, my thoughts wandered from one subject to another. I thought about the past school year, I thought about my sad summer on the island, and I thought about my future. Whenever I landed on Ace, I punched the Reset button. This summer wasn't about Ace. It was about me. It was about expanding my hunting grounds, about the possibility of meeting interesting single men who I might be interested in dating once my sabbatical ended, and about my reentry into the world of shag dancing. It was about testing my heart and testing my resistance to the wrong type of man.

Having paid little attention to my progress along the familiar route, seeing the bridge linking the mainland to the island surprised me. My newfound bravado sank as fast as a ship with a gaping hole in its hull. I lifted my foot from the gas pedal and tapped the brake. I could still turn around, go home, take a waitress job this summer to help pay off my credit card debt.

I took a deep breath and pressed down on the gas pedal. The front tires whirred onto the entrance ramp of the bridge. I could no longer turn around—at least until I was on the island.

But I'd be okay. I wouldn't be a captive there. I could leave anytime. And I was pretty sure it was time to start work on getting over my fear of having my heart broken again. And if I discovered I wasn't ready, I could leave the island with a clear conscience. Della liked having someone around she could count on, but she was capable of running the B and B on her own.

I turned my car onto the B and B's driveway.

Della was going up the porch steps with a plastic grocery bag in each hand. At the sound of my tires on the gravel parking area, she turned and waited for me to join her.

"Hey, Honey," Della said as I came up the porch steps. "Glad you're here. Get yourself and Bowser settled. Ace and Emily will be here in a half hour for lunch."

A series of shocks jolted my heart. I hadn't counted on seeing Ace before Saturday. And who was Emily?

I let Bowser out of the carrier. He bounded off toward the shrubs, rousting a bird from a low branch.

"Who's Emily?" I asked, trying for the breezy sound of not really caring about the answer.

"The person I hired to run the goat farm. Mr. Hereford told me last Thursday he'd be retiring at the end of this week and moving closer to his son."

"Lucky you found someone to replace him so soon."

"Ace was friends in college with one of Emily's brothers. He's known her for years. Her family raised goats."

"So why isn't she running her family's goat farm?"

"They sold their farm years ago and moved to Florida."

"To raise alligators?"

Della looked at me with feigned annoyance. "To help one of their daughters raise her six children."

"Raising alligators might have been easier."

Della laughed. "I've got to start lunch. Unless you have something else you need to do, come down to the kitchen once you get Bowser settled."

I called Bowser. He bounded up the porch steps. He was acting more exuberant than usual. I got him and our things stashed in our room and then checked my appearance. With my sunburn faded, I looked ghostly. I perked up my cheeks and lips with a light touch of rouge and lipstick and then headed to the kitchen.

Della's homemade spicy tomato soup perfumed the air.

I fixed myself a cup of hot tea. "Have you expanded your goat herd yet?" I asked.

"Emily's doing some research first. She's looking at our capacity and studying our marketing opportunities, and then she'll give me her opinion on the number of milk goats she thinks are practical."

"So she's business-smart too."

"She has a master's degree in business."

"Married?" I crossed my fingers.

"No."

I had to get over being jealous of single women who showed up in Ace's orbit.

My mouth dropped open.

It was jealousy, not annoyance over being ignored, I'd experienced during dinner with Marie and Ace. I gave myself an imaginary high five. Naming my true emotion was like lifting a fifty-pound weight off my chest.

Taking a break from men had allowed my defenses to settle like silt and opened up room for me to see the truth. This summer I'd be open to discovering how much more I'd gained. And whatever happened, I wouldn't run away. Good or bad, I'd face the truth and pay homage to my grandmother by dealing with it in a joyful and optimistic spirit.

Della handed me a loaf of her homemade bread, interrupting my self-absorbed rumination.

"Cut off eight thick slices, Honey."

"Has an arson investigator come around to talk to you about the fire?"

"No. But they brought in a dog and then sent something to a lab for testing."

"I doubt you need to worry."

"You never know, Honey. I'm feeling a little uneasy over this. Who besides me has a motive to set fire to the place?"

"Without a witness, arson is hard to pin on someone unless they find something at the scene to identify a suspect." I severed the loaf of bread into near equal halves. "How old is Emily?"

"Twenty-nine."

Twenty-nine, unmarried, a goat expert, and business-smart. "I hope she and I can be friends."

"She'll be pretty busy at the farm and won't have much social time for a while. But I think you'll like her."

I cut the eight slices off the loaf of bread and then looked around. "What else can I help with?"

"You can set the kitchen table. And then the pan of lemon bars needs cutting."

Della began buttering the bread slices on one side.

The creak of the front door and then male and female laughter heralded the arrival of Ace and Emily.

I looked up from the plate of lemon bars I was holding. A female with blond hair, big eyes, long legs, and a great body stood next to Ace in the doorway opening. I wanted to cut my heart out right then and there. Not only was Emily goat-savvy and business-smart, she was the type of woman men notice.

"Hey, Honey," Ace said. "Smells good, Della."

I froze. The only thing I could manage was a small bob of my head.

Ace looked at me and knit his brows. "Honey, Emily Wainwright." He turned to look at Emily. "Emily, Honey Benton."

Emily stepped forward, extending her hand. "Hi."

I set the plate on the counter, wiped my hands on my shorts, and took her hand. Emily's fingers were long and tapered. Her grip was firm but gentle. The perfect hands and touch for milking goats—I supposed. But she was not the type one took a dislike to right off the bat. Her smile seemed genuine. Her eyes were free of anything other than a sincere interest in meeting me.

"Hi. I'm Della's niece and assistant for the summer and Ace's shag dance partner." Like my earlier insistence on Bowser's title being recognized, I'd blurted out all of my current titles that gave me rank.

Emily smiled, giving me a glimpse of perfect teeth. "I'm happy to meet you. All Ace talked about on our drive over here was his new shag dance partner."

Really? I thought I caught a fleeting look of dismay in Ace's eyes.

"What do you do the rest of the year?" she asked.

"I teach third grade. In Farmington."

"One of my sisters teaches fifth grade in Belmont."

Della was working at the stove with her back to us. "Ten more minutes and lunch will be ready," she said.

Ace moved to the stove and peered over Della's shoulder. "Looks good," he said. "Emily and I'll be on the deck. The storm moving up the coast is creating big waves. It's quite a sight."

He strode to the rear of the kitchen and pushed the sliding glass door open. Emily followed him out to the deck. From my position at the counter, I had a clear view of them standing at the rail looking out toward the ocean. They were standing so close their shoulders touched.

If I did decide to have a summer fling to test my readiness to search for the right man, it didn't look like Ace would be available. And I'd need to work at keeping a joyful spirit. Della must have sensed my dismay. She came over and put an arm around my shoulders. "Never discount your talents, Honey."

I scooped the last lemon bar from the pan and dropped it on the plate.

Joyful and *optimistic* were my watchwords for the summer. If I got caught up in an undertow of despair at every setback, I'd undermine the confidence I'd been working on gaining.

"Is there anything else I can do?" I asked with an upbeat tone in my voice.

"Let Emily and Ace know lunch is ready."

Della cut each of the grilled sandwiches into halves and layered them on a plate. She set the plate on the table, picked up a soup bowl, and took it to the stove.

I pushed open the slider. Now they were not only standing shoulder to shoulder, they were standing hip to hip. Ace was pointing to something in the distance. Emily laughed a soft feminine laugh.

"Lunch," I yelled. I didn't sound joyful. I didn't sound feminine. I attempted a laugh, but it sounded more like I was being strangled. "Come in before the soup gets cold," I added, sounding like a harassed mother or a peevish wife.

Ace turned. "Honey, come look at this."

I stepped out to the rail.

My effort at command and control had been ignored exactly as it had been when he'd delivered the cheese to my door. And like always, I'd complied with his command. This summer would be challenging.

At the lifeguard station down the beach, a yellow caution flag fluttered in the wind. A surfer rose up out of the water, caught a wave, and rode it toward shore—racing ahead of the breaking water. I ignored my own command to come in for lunch before the soup got cold and watched until the wave swallowed the surfer and coughed him up again.

Another surfer caught a wave.

"Della will be mad if we don't go in," I said, sounding like a petulant child this time.

Ace laughed. "And making Della mad is the last thing one should do if they value their head. The woman wields a mean spatula."

Emily laughed along with Ace. "I'll remember," she said.

"Ace is kidding, Emily. Della is the sweetest person in the world," I said.

After Della sorted everyone into chairs, I kept my gaze focused on the table. Everyone ate for a while without speaking.

I set aside my sandwich and dipped my spoon into my bowl of soup. My throat was so tight, swallowing liquid was difficult. I swirled the soup around the bowl.

Della wiped her lips with a napkin. "Emily, did you have any problem moving in? Is there anything you need?"

Emily put her spoon down. "Everything's been great. Ace helped unload my car and then he replaced the burned-out lightbulb in the bathroom."

I filled my spoon and took a tiny sip. My sour mood made Della's soup taste sour. I stopped eating.

"I forgot to let Bowser out," I said, and got up from the table so fast I knocked over my chair. Jealousy, even named, was not an easy emotion to control and made it impossible to maintain a joyful and optimistic mood.

I righted the chair.

Ace stood and reached into the right front pocket of his jeans. "I brought Bowser another treat from Riff's."

"Thanks."

Ace remained standing and looked right at me. I steeled

myself to keep my eyes focused on him. "After lunch, Della wants to talk business with Emily. Maybe you and Bowser will join me on the porch and I can give him his treat."

"Sure."

I went up the stairs feeling defeated. I wasn't handling this well at all. I opened my bedroom door. Bowser greeted me with quick snaps of his tail. I bent to scratch his head. He licked my chin. His show of affection gave me the boost I needed to dump the self-doubt threatening to ruin the first day of my summer.

I followed Bowser down the stairs and told myself if I had a crush on Ace, fine. It doesn't mean I have to get all tangled up if he didn't have a crush on me. "Enjoy the moment," I murmured.

At the front door, Bowser stopped, sniffed, and looked around. "He's here," I said. "But you can stop worrying about him being competition for my heart—if that's the reason you don't like him."

I opened the front door. Bowser bolted through and went down the porch steps. He headed for the line of rhododendron bushes. He came back up the steps and sat down next to my chair.

Ace came out to the porch. I picked Bowser up. Ace chose a rocking chair on the opposite side of the porch.

Bowser didn't bark, and he didn't growl. Now what?

"Catch, Honey," Ace said.

I turned my head in his direction and then made a nimble catch of the plastic bag he tossed at me.

Bowser jumped down. He waited for me to take out a biscuit and give it to him. But before he began enjoying his treat, he looked over at Ace and began wagging his tail in his "I love you" wave.

"You're welcome, my man." Ace gave Bowser a salute and

then commenced rocking. "So, Honey, can you practice this afternoon?" His tone was neutral, as if the question were a spur of the moment thought.

"I'll have to check with Della."

Bowser had stretched out next to my rocker. I went inside.

Della and Emily were still sitting at the kitchen table. I started to clear off the dishes. "Ace wants to know if I'm free to practice this afternoon." I set the empty lemon bar plate in the sink.

"Sure. All the guests are checked out, and Ace helped clean the rooms this morning, so they're done. I expect the new arrivals will have checked in by seven. I shouldn't need help until tomorrow morning."

"Okay, I'll clean the kitchen before I leave."

"It's a deal. I need to go over some numbers with Emily. We'll move to my office and get out of your way."

I went back to the porch. Bowser was sitting in Ace's lap getting his head scratched.

I'd been here for less than a day and the minute I stepped out of my car, things had started going downhill. And now my loyal dog had abandoned me, his affections bought with a couple of gourmet dog biscuits. It should be a felony to bribe a dog to gain his friendship.

"I see Bowser no longer hates you," I said, sounding huffy despite trying for an offhand tone of voice. "It's time for his afternoon nap." I walked over and snatched Bowser out of Ace's lap. "I'm free to practice this afternoon. Say when and where and I'll be there."

"Sam's Grill. Twenty minutes. Sam's letting us use the room at the rear of the grill."

"I know where Sam's is. Thirty minutes. I volunteered to clean up the kitchen."

"Good, I'll help you." Ace rose from the rocker.

Bowser, in a show of adoration for a previous enemy, licked Ace's hand.

Had Bowser understood what I'd said when I'd assured him he didn't have to worry about Ace replacing him? Why else would he leave me unprotected from this man?

"How long have you known Emily?" I asked as we went inside.

"A long time."

"She's very attractive."

"Yup. And smart."

"Can you hold Bowser while I set up the gate so he can't get into the food areas? I'll take him back upstairs as soon as the kitchen's cleaned up."

Ace held out his arms. I handed Bowser to him.

"I almost had him signed up for the Resistance before you came back to the porch."

"What did you offer him as a signing bonus? A daily supply of Riff's dog biscuits?" My tone wasn't joyful now either.

"Sorry, but all information about the Resistance is classified top secret," Ace said with a smile.

If our practice was to go well, I needed to lighten up my mood. "Maybe I'll join too," I said with an upbeat lilt in my voice.

"Can't. Males only."

"What does the Resistance resist?"

"Only members are entitled to know what the mission is."

"I don't think my dog is available," I said with a smile.

Ace smiled back. He looked confident he'd win.

What chance did I have if gourmet dog biscuits were all it took to seduce Bowser into falling into Ace's arms? How little would it take for Ace to breach my weakened lines of defense— if he wanted to? Not much, I feared.

I was on my own.

I got the gate in place. Ace let Bowser down. Della and Emily were no longer in the kitchen. Ace wiped off the table and then began scrubbing the pans.

A man who could cook and clean deserved respect. I put a soup bowl in the bottom dishwasher rack.

When we'd finished, Ace leaned back against the sink, looked around the kitchen, and nodded his approval. "You and I make a good kitchen cleanup team too. Now let's go dance."

"I'll meet you there. I need to get my shoes and comb my hair and get Bowser upstairs."

Ace crossed his arms over his chest. He skewed his lips and studied my face for a few seconds. "I'll wait on the porch."

Like Bowser, Ace had a keen sense of people and of dogs too. I was pretty sure he knew I was nervous about spending time alone with him and was determined to make it difficult for me to make excuses.

Ace went out the front door.

I picked up Bowser. "How could you?" I hissed through clamped teeth. "By befriending the enemy, you left my flanks unprotected."

Bowser made a soft snuffle.

I started up the stairs. If I couldn't trust my dog, whom could I trust? My grandmother must have been born without the sorrowful and pessimistic emotions, because it wasn't possible to be joyful and optimistic all the time if one had the opposing emotions to deal with.

Bowser went straight to his bed. I found my dance shoes, ran a brush through my hair, and hurried down the stairs. The sooner I got through this, the sooner I'd get back here to call up my reserves—if I could find any.

* * *

Sam's Grill was busy. Ace waved to the burly, bald-headed man behind the counter. The man waved back. We made our way across the dining area. Ace introduced me to Sam. Sam handed Ace a key and winked at me. "Keep it. Use the space whenever you want," Sam said. "Nice to meet you, Honey. Good luck on Saturday."

"Thanks."

The door to our practice room was around back.

Ace got the door open and gestured for me to enter. Light streamed in from the row of narrow windows set high in the wall. The floor was wood. I could feel the air-conditioning.

"Nice," I said as I turned to face Ace. He was standing in the doorway with his arms and legs crossed and one shoulder pressed against the doorframe. I hated it when he did that. For some reason, his casual but closed-off pose tugged at my heart.

Ace straightened up and came inside. "This room used to have a door to the Grill. Sam's predecessor had live bands and dances here during the big tourist months. But he didn't draw a big enough crowd to make it worth the trouble. Sam closed up the door and then tried to rent it out for private parties. That didn't work either, so this part of the building isn't used for much."

"Things work out funny sometimes," I said.

"Yup, more often than not." Ace walked over to a table that held a CD player. He pushed the Play button.

There was a long pause before the music started, giving us time to get into the start position.

"Let's stick with the basics for a while," Ace said. "Get to know each other's style. You can begin learning my signals."

He took my hand and put his arm around my waist. Ripples of tingly prickles ran from my fingertips to my shoulder. I nodded to let Ace know sticking to the basics was fine with me.

In shag dancing, the male always leads. It was up to me to respond to Ace, mirror his steps if he wanted me to, or continue the basic steps as he performed variations. The night of Cameronfest he'd stayed with steps that were pretty basic. At that level of competition, it had been enough.

Our practice session went well. Ace showed off a couple of advanced steps for me to work on. At the higher levels of competition we'd need a more complicated routine, and I'd have to mirror him with precision.

When practice was over, Ace said he had to get back to the goat farm. I walked back to the B and B, still unsettled over Bowser's traitorous behavior, Emily's superior everything, and most of all my physical attraction to Ace.

As I climbed up the B and B steps, Harry called a greeting as he passed me on his way down. "Good luck on Saturday," he called over his shoulder.

"Thanks," I called back without much energy

I got Bowser and took him to the beach. I couldn't be angry with Bowser for siding with Ace. Bowser wouldn't understand. We walked along the sand in the direction of Miss Crandell's house. When we got there, I knocked on her door.

The instant Hattie opened the door, she grinned. "Why, Miss Honey, this very morning Miss Crandell was recalling the day you and Mr. Ace came to lunch. She said we need to put our heads together to figure out how to get y'all to come back again." Hattie stepped to one side. "Come say hello."

"I'd be happy to come visit anytime Della doesn't need me." I pointed at Bowser. "Would Miss Crandell like to meet my dog, or should I leave him out here?"

Hattie looked down. Boswer's tail was flying from one side to the other so fast it blurred. "Miss Crandell, she's got a soft spot for dogs. Been two years since her beloved CeCe passed on. I do believe she'd be happy to meet this fine-looking dog."

I bent down to pick Bowser up and carried him into the living room. Miss Crandell was dozing in her wing chair.

Hattie nudged Miss Crandell's shoulder. "Look who's come to visit," she said.

Miss Crandell opened her eyes. Her gaze settled on Bowser. "Well, my stars, what a handsome dog."

I couldn't see his face, but if I knew Bowser, he was showing his doggy grin.

"And Honey too. How nice of you to come visit."

"Bowser and I were taking a walk on the beach. I thought he'd enjoy meeting you."

Miss Crandell held out her arms. I set Bowser down on her lap.

"Do sit down, Honey." She stroked Bowser's back as she gestured to an armless wooden chair placed close to her wing chair.

"How is Ace?" she asked, without looking at me. "We haven't seen him since you were here to lunch."

"He might be fearful you and Hattie have more surprises up your sleeves."

Miss Crandell laughed. "How I do love that child. Wallace was a good boy. And he's become a good man."

Wallace? I tucked this information away. It could come in handy at the right time.

"We've been practicing shag dance steps. On Saturday we're competing again. If you give me a date and time convenient for you and Hattie, I'll try to get him to come with me for a visit."

"Well, glory be." Miss Crandell's eyes twinkled. "Hattie, did you hear?"

Hattie giggled. "I did, Miss Crandell."

It was obvious they had Ace in their mischief scopes.

I stood and picked up Bowser. If it would make Miss Crandell and Hattie happy, I'd work on getting Ace to visit them again.

"Let me know when you want me to bring Ace around. I'll do my best."

Hattie let me out, shaking her head and clucking her tongue. "An answer to a prayer," she muttered to herself. "And be sure to bring Bowser next time you stop by," she said in her normal voice.

Hattie filled the open doorway, waving.

I felt renewed, serene, and balanced again, my emotions back under control. Tomorrow when Ace and I practiced in the room at Sam's where we were isolated from the world, it wouldn't be such an emotion-churning event.

The next afternoon, Ace taught me a new step. We worked on putting together the routine for Saturday's competition and at perfecting the mirroring of our footwork.

We took a break. Ace had brought a small cooler. He pulled out two sodas and handed me one. I took a long drink of the cold liquid and then lowered the bottle.

"Bowser and I stopped at Miss Crandell's yesterday. She and Hattie would love for you to visit again. I promised them, if they'd let me know a day and time, I'd see to it you got there."

Ace leaned back against the table where the CD player sat. He gripped the table's edge with both hands and crossed his legs at the ankles.

Not a friendly response.

"What do you think they're up to?" he asked, looking pensive.

I pursed my lips as I watched his face. "Do you have any idea the amount of pleasure hoodwinking you into coming to lunch on your birthday gave them?"

His lips turned up into a faint smile. "Yeah. But it didn't amuse me. I gave up celebrating my birthday years ago."

"And maybe the expression of their love for you touched an emotion you don't want touched."

Good grief. Why had I opened up this can of worms?

Ace turned his back to me, unplugged the CD player, and gathered up his CDs. I went out the door. I didn't look back. What happened to our partnership after this was up to Ace.

The parlor of the B and B had the quiet air of a space empty of all living things. I peeked into Della's office. She wasn't there. I headed to the kitchen. She wasn't there either. I retrieved Bowser and took him to the beach, my sanctuary and his playground.

At least it had been my sanctuary.

Ace was sitting on the sand dune in front of the B and B.

Bowser took off and sat down next to him.

I walked past—ignoring them both. The last thing I needed in my life was a man so emotionally scarred he couldn't be open to the kindness of others. And the fact Bowser had bonded with him wasn't enough to disregard this. Bowser loved all kinds of people and let all kinds of people love him in return.

I continued across the sand to the section of the beach where the waves kept the sand wet and packed, making it easier to walk. I headed toward the pier with a purposeful stride.

I'd promised Della I'd be here for the summer, I'd promised myself this summer would be a good time to test my heart, and I wasn't about to run—yet—but at the moment, I didn't think summer could end soon enough.

At home, once I was settled into my familiar and stable world, I might begin working on my master's degree, or I might take a waitress job at night and save up for a trip to Italy or France or both. If I wanted to, I'd extend my sabbatical for five years, travel, get my master's, and maybe even start performing again.

I heard a bark. Bowser ran up beside me. I stopped and knelt down. "Do you have any idea how much your disloyalty hurts me?"

Bowser appeared puzzled.

A shadow loomed over us. I looked up. Ace was looking down, his eyes clouded. His expression was grim.

He held out his hand to help me stand. "I'm sorry, Honey. Can we practice again tomorrow?"

I looked out at the water, studying the swells. No matter what obstacles the ocean encountered, the water found a way around—or in some cases over—and continued its journey toward shore.

Ace was trying.

I could try too.

"Sure." I wasn't ready to apologize to him yet. Maybe later.

He gave me a quick smile. "Let me know when Hattie and Miss Crandell want us to come for a visit. I'll be there."

He turned and started jogging back toward the D and D. Bowser stayed at my heels as I kept going toward the pier with my head down and my patched heart beginning to crack.

On Saturday Ace picked me up for the competition in Millersville. Having had time to think about tonight's competition, and knowing how much doing well meant to Ace, I was more nervous than I'd been on the night of the Cameronfest competition.

"Do you know any of the couples we're competing against tonight?" I asked.

"Not personally. But I've heard most of their names before."

"Regulars, huh?"

"Yup."

He turned onto Highway 17 and headed north. I put my hands in my lap and wove my fingers together to prevent them from making nervous little taps.

Ace glanced at my hands. "We'll do fine, Honey. We don't have to win."

"I like to win." Another truth. Another sign of my progress.

Ace laughed. "Me too." He pulled out and passed a tractor. "I'm going to use my winnings from Cameronfest for a welcome-home dinner with my stepbrother. He's in Iraq."

Ace went around a slow-moving car and then got back into the right lane. "How about you?"

A sense of guilt replaced my nervousness. I should have donated my winnings to the no-kill shelter. "I bought a new swimsuit."

"Great. When the waves are right, you want to go boogie boarding with me?"

"Thanks. I think I'll stick to dancing."

He laughed a sweet laugh. "We should be there in ten minutes. If you want to eat first, we've got plenty of time."

"I'm too nervous to eat, but coffee would be great."

Ace pulled his car into the parking lot of a fast-food place.

Twenty minutes later we were in line to sign in. Competitors and the people who came to watch trickled into the venue where the event was taking place. I eyed the couples we'd be competing against.

One couple looked familiar.

I looked closer.

Sam Harkin and Betty Shaw. They'd been part of my college group. I started toward them to say hello. As soon as they saw me, they broke into big smiles.

"Honey," Sam called. "You and Jared back on the circuit?"

I gave Betty a hug and then turned to Sam. "I haven't been with Jared for a long time. Come meet my new partner."

"You divorced?"

"Never married."

Betty took my hand. "I'm sorry, Honey."

"So was I for a while, but our breakup ended up being a blessing."

Ace came over to join us. I made the introductions. Sam and Ace bonded right away. Betty looked at me and lifted her eyebrows. I mouthed the word "no."

Sam and Betty said they'd moved back to South Carolina the year before and had started competing again two weeks after the move. Unless they'd lost some of their skill while they were away, they'd be hard to beat.

The announcer took the stage. We wished each other luck.

All the competitors tonight were far more skilled than those who'd competed at Cameronfest. Sam and Betty took first place. Ace and I placed third. Ace gave me a peck on the lips. I didn't know which thrilled me more—Ace and I placing third in a group of world-class shag dancers or the fact he'd kissed me—even if his kiss expressed nothing but his excitement over how well we'd done.

On the drive home, Ace dissected each of the other couple's strengths and weaknesses. He came to the conclusion that if we could beat Sam and Betty, we had a good shot at qualifying and even winning Nationals. He talked about adding two advanced steps to our routine.

I listened, murmuring my agreement every now and then. I loved Ace's enthusiasm for perfecting our dancing. Not only did we dance well together, we were both determined competitors, and tonight we had proven we could compete at the top levels. But to continue dancing with Ace, I had to keep my heart from getting tangled up and creating hazards—like jealousy.

Ace turned his car onto the driveway of the B and B. He parked, got out, and walked me to the door. And this time, before I could say good night, he kissed me. For real.

His lips were as soft as I'd imagined they would be. He deepened the kiss, parting his lips.

My toes tingled. Bolts of pleasure traveled up my spine. I broke it off as soon as I could manage and took a quick couple of steps back.

"I think we'll do better as dance partners if we don't kiss." I hoped he hadn't heard the breathless trembling in my voice.

"Sorry, Honey. I've been trying for a long time to find a partner who fits so well." His eyes caught mine. "Next time we place or win, I promise I'll keep my emotional fervor in check."

I grabbed hold of the doorknob and turned it. "I'm glad you and Sam hit it off. My ex and I used to beat Sam and Betty sometimes."

Ace narrowed his beautiful eyes—the sea-green color deepened because of the lack of light on the porch. "Sorry I let you down tonight."

I reached out my hand and placed a finger across his lips. "That isn't what I meant, Ace. Sam and Betty have been dancing together since they were in their teens. I only meant you and I can beat them too."

He laughed. "If you have time, we'll add a half hour more to our daily practice."

"I—"

Ace didn't wait to hear if I agreed to more practice time. Instead, he turned and dashed down the steps, calling good night over his shoulder. I stood there while his car went down the drive, watching the taillights until they were no longer visible. And then I caught my breath and sighed.

When I finally went inside, noises were coming from the kitchen. I went to see if Della wanted some help.

She was cooking and singing along with the songs playing on the radio.

"Hey, Honey, how'd it go?" she asked. She cracked an egg and dumped the contents from the shell into a bowl. "My overnight breakfast casserole," she said.

"Ace and I came in third." I filled a glass with water.

"Ace must have been thrilled."

I took a long sip. "A couple I used to compete against came in first."

"Shag dancing's a small world," Della said.

"Hmm." I was still reeling from the effects of Ace's second kiss and didn't really want to get into a long conversation with Della.

"Is there anything I can do?"

"Not until morning, thanks, Honey. Are you going to continue the partnership?"

"One day at a time."

Della boomed a laugh and then placed the contents of a package of sausage into a skillet and turned on the burner. "I fed Bowser his supper and took him out a half hour ago," she said.

"Thanks, Della. I'm exhausted. See you in the morning."

Della glanced at me with unasked questions in her eyes. She knew me well enough to know I was leaving out something big. I'd tell her—but not until after I figured out if Ace kissing me had made it impossible for me to continue dancing with him.

And something even more troubling about Ace kept nagging at me. I hadn't been wrong when I put him in the player category. In the short time I'd known him, he'd beguiled Marie, been more than friendly with Emily, and now he'd kissed me twice—in one night. On the positive side, I was pretty sure I didn't have to worry about him kissing me again.

He wouldn't want to risk losing his winning partner.

I climbed into bed and turned out the light.

Tomorrow, I'd worry about my heart.

Tonight, I'd savor Ace's last kiss.

* * *

A loud whirring sound woke me. Red lights flashed across my windows.

Bowser jumped on my bed and barked.

Fire trucks.

I leaped out of bed, put my robe on, and hurried down the stairs. Della and several of the B and B's guests were on the porch. The sky had an eerie red glow. Through the trees, I could see the circling fire engine light. The smell of wood burning assaulted my nose.

"What's on fire?" I asked.

"The house that burned before," Della said.

We all stood out there in our nightclothes, captivated by the sight, the sounds, and the smell of this unsettling event.

Bowser rubbed against my leg. I reached down to pick him up. "It's okay. The firemen are putting out the fire."

He nestled closer.

The guests all drifted back to their rooms. Della and I went inside.

The phone in her office rang. I waited in the front room while she answered.

Seconds later she dashed out of her office. Her eyes were huge, her lips tight. "They've arrested Ace. I've got to bail him out," she said as she went up the stairs two at a time.

Bowser began barking in earnest. I hurried up the stairs after Della. "Arrested for what?"

"Arson."

My heart was in my throat. I struggled to breathe as I dashed up the stairs. On the hall stair landing, Bowser ran in circles. "I'm coming too!" I shouted.

I got into street clothes and went down the stairs with Bowser at my heels.

Della's car-door locks clicked open.

We piled into her car.

She broke the island's twenty-five-mile-per-hour speed limit as she headed to the police station with its attached jail.

Ace was sitting on a bench in a cell. A smudge of soot streaked his forehead and cheek.

Della put up the bail money.

The sheriff released Ace into Della's custody.

Bowser sat on Ace's lap the entire way back to the B and B.

Ace and I sat in rocking chairs on the porch while Della went to make coffee. Bowser looked over at me for a second and then jumped into Ace's lap. I had no idea what to say, so I didn't say anything. Ace didn't say anything either.

Della returned with the coffee. "What happened, Ace?" she asked.

"I couldn't sleep, so I went for a walk. I got within a few feet of the house and smelled smoke. I went around back to see if I should call the fire department. When I got to the backyard, a person standing in the shadows tossed a metal can at me and then ran. I took off after them and tripped over something. When I picked myself up, they were gone."

"Could you identify the person?"

"I'm pretty sure it was a male, but I couldn't see his face well enough to say for sure."

"How did you end up getting arrested?"

"I was standing on the side of the road trying to get my cell phone out of my pocket to call the fire department. Joe drove up in his police car, took one sniff, and hauled me off to jail. Claims not only did I smell of gasoline, but I have a motive."

"What motive?"

"Maybe he thinks I'm trying to prevent another B and B from opening on the island."

Della got to her feet. "I'll drive you home."

Ace set Bowser on the porch and then got out of the rocker.

"This has been a crazy twenty-four hours," he said, glancing over at me. "I hope my impulsive actions tonight won't have long-term consequences."

I think he winked at me, but there wasn't enough light to know for sure.

I stayed on the porch, waiting for Della to return.

She was back fifteen minutes later. She parked and then came up the porch steps and sat in the rocker next to mine. The porch boards creaked as we rocked. A breeze, carrying a faint scent of burning wood, played with the wind chimes on a nearby property.

Della laid her hand on mine. "Ace used to live in the house someone's trying to burn down."

Would painful memories of living there cause him to try to burn it down?

Della stood up and yawned. "Six o'clock isn't far away. We need to get back to sleep."

With Ace in trouble, and my lips still on fire from the memory of his kiss, my getting back to sleep could take a while.

Chapter Eight

My alarm woke me. I had fallen asleep without any trouble after all. I got dressed, got Bowser settled, and went to help with breakfast.

Marie called at six thirty. She'd picked up her engagement ring yesterday afternoon and wanted to know if she could come to the island today to show it to me. I told her I couldn't wait to see it. She said she'd be here around three.

I hung up, feeling gloomy. Seeing an engagement ring on Marie's finger would solidify the fact that she and Jeff were getting married and nothing would change her mind. Not that who Marie married was any of my business, but she'd been my best friend for a long time, and I'd be sad if she weren't happy.

Besides, I'd miss her more than I wanted to admit.

I told Della that Marie would be coming today and why.

"You're worried about her, aren't you?" Della asked.

"Sort of."

Della took her breakfast casserole out of the oven and set the hot dish on a trivet. "My advice is not to say a single negative word about Jeff. If Marie finds out later she's made a mistake and ends up in divorce court, she won't forgive you."

"I know. A couple of years ago, I suggested she might want to give up on Jeff. She didn't speak to me for a week."

Della turned and looked at me. "Nothing anyone said would have convinced me I was wrong about my ex. People have to learn some things on their own."

Didn't I know the truth of this? Failing to see the obvious and falling in love with the wrong man again was my biggest worry. "I'll pray I'm wrong about Marie and Jeff."

"Good. And if it turns out you're right, don't ever say I tried to tell you."

I laughed. "I'll write your advice on sticky notes and put them in various places at home and at school to remind myself."

Murmurs of conversation could be heard in the breakfast area. I carried in the pitcher of orange juice.

Two couples were talking about last night's fire.

I set the pitcher on the table. "It's the second time the place has caught fire. They suspect arson."

The guests who had come in gasped.

I heard the information being repeated as more of the guests came in.

It had added a spark of excitement to the ocean's mellow and calming atmosphere.

Fifteen minutes before I'd planned on leaving for Sam's for our scheduled practice, Ace showed up at the B and B.

Della came out of her office to say hello.

Bowser, who had sprawled on the rug in the parlor, jumped to his feet and ran to greet Ace.

Ace bent down to speak my dog. "Your lordship," Ace said. "The Resistance has been assigned an important mission."

Della laughed her joyful laugh. "To find the arsonist?"

Ace stood up, his expression sober. "They found the container that was tossed at me and lifted a couple of good fingerprints. They've sent them to the state crime lab."

"So what's the mission?" I asked.

"Shag dance practice is called off for today. Bowser and I will call on Miss Crandell and Hattie instead."

"Bowser cannot go without me."

"Fine. Most armies have camp followers."

"Well, I—"

Ace smiled. "In the virtuous meaning of the phrase."

"Oh, well then"—I lifted my chin—"I assure you, if I have to defend myself, I can shoot straight."

Good, Honey. Don't let Ace think he controls you or your dog.

Ace looked at me with twinkling eyes and laughed. "I don't think shooting will be necessary. Miss Crandell and Hattie are wily opponents, but their operations are conducted without the use of deadly weapons."

I laughed as a burst of joy and optimism replaced my gloomy pessimism over Marie's engagement.

Keeping the leash taut, Bowser led the way to Miss Crandell's.

She and Hattie were on the porch. Hattie got to her feet and then waited for us at the top of the porch steps with her fists pressed into the flesh of her ample hips.

"Why, look who's come to visit," Hattie said, followed by her joyful laugh. She stepped aside as Bowser mounted the steps. "Look here, Miss Crandell."

Miss Crandell held out her hands to Bowser. "We are honored to have a member of the aristocracy come visit us," she said.

"And an officer in the Resistance Corps," Ace added.

Miss Crandell saluted and chuckled.

Hattie gazed toward the heavens.

I removed Bowser's leash and lifted him into Miss Crandell's lap. He licked her face. Her eyes lit up.

"Sit down, you two," Hattie said. "I'll be right back."

Hattie returned with a pitcher of lemonade, four drinking glasses, and a plate of homemade cookies. She set the tray on the table next to her chair and filled the glasses. She handed them around, passed the plate of cookies, and then picked up her own glass and sat down.

Miss Crandell fed Bowser pieces of cookie. "How is dance practice going?" she asked Ace.

"Great," he said.

"I'm glad you found each other," she said. "I loved dancing in my day. I met some of the best people."

Hattie offered the plate of cookies again. "Y'all hear about the burned house getting set afire again?"

The house was across the street and two houses down from theirs.

"We slept right through all the commotion," Miss Crandell said. "We didn't know a thing about it till a neighbor dropped in this morning." She took a second cookie and broke off a piece for Bowser. "When Ace lived in that house, we'd sit out here and see him come and go," Miss Crandell said.

Since I already knew Ace had lived there, Hattie's statement didn't surprise me. I kept up the slow steady rhythm of my rocking chair and then stole a glance at Ace. He was gazing at something far beyond the porch.

If he ever wanted to talk about his childhood memories when I was around, he'd have to begin without my asking questions.

"He sho' kept himself busy," Hattie added, looking over at Ace and shaking her head from side to side.

Ace frowned and leaned back in his chair. "That was a long time ago," he said in a voice void of discernible emotion. And then he grinned, sat forward, and held out his empty glass.

"Your lemonade is the world's best, Hattie," he said. She poured the last of the lemonade into his glass. "I used to drink enough of Hattie's lemonade every week to fill a bathtub."

"Not to mention the dozens of cookies you ate," Miss Crandell added. "Hattie and I had to bake a fresh batch of cookies every day of the week to keep up."

Next thing, I'd become the subject of their reminiscence—and I had plenty of my own memories I didn't want stirred up right now.

I stopped rocking and stood up. "I'm sorry to leave so soon," I said. "My friend Marie is coming for a visit today to show me her engagement ring." I unwound Bowser's leash. "Thanks for welcoming us and for the lemonade and cookies."

Ace stood up too. Hattie held out the cookie plate and insisted he take the last cookie.

I hugged Hattie and started over to kiss Miss Crandell's cheek and retrieve Bowser.

"I hear the two of you have stirred up quite a fire," Miss Crandell said as I bent down to give her a quick kiss.

I straightened up and looked at Ace. He averted his eyes, took Bowser's leash from my hand, and clipped it to the dog's collar.

"Come along, my man," Ace said.

Bowser gave Miss Crandell's hand a lick and then jumped down.

"Y'all come visit us again real soon," Hattie said, as she slapped her knee with her hand.

"Do," Miss Crandell said. "Anytime. And be mindful of fires."

Ace bent down and kissed Miss Crandell on the cheek.

Hattie got to her feet. He gave Hattie a big hug. "Visiting you is always a treat," he said. "And a challenge."

Ace spun around, and then he and Bowser double-timed it down the porch steps. I hurried to catch up and finally did at the end of the drive. "What's the hurry?" I asked.

"Emily's making cheese today. I told her I'd help."

"Oh," I said, sounding as deflated as I felt.

So Ace had canceled dance practice today so he could help Emily. He should have just said so. I realized jealousy would be a recurring emotion I'd have to deal with. And I didn't know how exactly. I wanted to tell Ace that making cheese wouldn't help him become a shag dance champion, and an hour and a half of lost practice time could make the difference between our winning and losing.

But I didn't.

Instead, I kept enough distance between us to avoid touching him and concentrated on keeping my true emotions from showing.

I sneaked a glance at Ace. He was looking straight ahead.

The three of us started up the drive of the B and B. I was relieved to see the guest parking area was empty except for Ace's car. I could use some quiet time to try to dig joyous up from under my layer of gloom.

Ace handed me Bowser's leash. I said good-bye. He nodded, got into his car, and drove off without waving.

I walked up the porch steps lost in thought. Ace clamming up and becoming pensive for a few seconds after Miss Crandell mentioned he'd lived in the half-burned house had been a telling moment. The fingerprints they'd lifted from the container might point to a suspect, but they wouldn't prove who the arsonist was. It seemed improbable that Ace would try to burn the place down to erase any childhood demons. But people no one would suspect did strange things all the time.

On the table by the front door I found a note from Della. She'd gone out to the farm to make a decision about a new piece of equipment. Bowser and I went up to our room.

I set my alarm to wake me in an hour.

Marie showed up on schedule. She had a gleaming one-carat diamond solitaire in a platinum setting on her ring finger.

A plus in Jeff's favor.

I fixed glasses of sweet tea and put two of the leftover scones from breakfast on a plate.

We took ourselves and the refreshments out to the deck. A sedate ocean and a cloudless sky greeted us.

Marie, wearing a pair of cutoff shorts and a halter top, stretched out in one of the lounge chairs. "It's so beautiful and peaceful here, Honey. I'm green with envy."

"I'm glad I'm working here this summer. It's been better than I'd expected."

Marie broke off a piece of a scone. "Anything going on with Ace?" She glanced over at me and popped the piece into her mouth.

"No." I changed the subject. "Have you and Jeff chosen a date for the wedding?"

"June. The first Saturday after school's out. Jeff said by not rushing it, I'd have time to hire the best vendors, plan our perfect honeymoon, and book the venues I want. His mother insists we send an invitation to every one of their relatives, no matter how distant the connection, all of their longtime acquaintances, all of the dealership's employees, and all of their regular customers. She handed me a list with two hundred and fifty-three names on it."

I sipped from my glass and vowed not to say anything negative about Marie's future mother-in-law either.

"Honey, please say you'll be my maid of honor. I know you hate standing around in an ugly dress at a boring reception, but you will—won't you?"

"Of course I will. I'd have been crushed if you didn't ask."

Marie breathed out a long sigh. "I promise you can choose the attendants' dresses. I have to ask Jeff's sister to be my matron of honor and his three female cousins to be bridesmaids, and I'm going to ask Chloe and Renee if they'll be bridesmaids."

I rattled the ice in my glass. Good luck on my getting to choose the dresses. Chloe and Renee were my friends too and would be on my side, but Jeff's mother would have four on her side plus herself. "That's a good start," I said. "How are your mom and dad?"

"Disappointed. Our church isn't big enough for the number of guests we're inviting, so the wedding will be at Jeff's church."

I caught a resigned wistfulness in Marie's voice. Not only would I refrain from saying anything negative about Jeff and about his mother, I wouldn't say anything negative about their wedding plans either. My prime duty, as Marie's maid of honor, was being the head cheerleader for the bride's team. "I'm really excited for you, Marie. Whatever you need me to do, just ask."

Marie and I had an early dinner at Bailey's Deli and then bought one of those giant bride magazines at the drugstore. Back at the B and B, we sat beneath the umbrella shading the table on the deck and leafed through the pages, studying the ads and looking at the photos. We circled things we liked and crossed out the things we didn't. Marie talked about where she'd like to go on her honeymoon. But it wouldn't surprise me to learn Jeff's mother dictated their honeymoon destination. And I didn't think the odds of choosing the flowers and the cake were in

Marie's favor either. I didn't doubt the reception would be at a place of his mother's choosing and the menu would be whatever his mother wanted. Marie would be lucky if she had the final say on her wedding dress.

Making a concentrated effort, I kept a smile on my face even as the hint of joyful optimism I'd strived to maintain seeped away. I made a set of rules for myself. If Marie complained, I'd listen and make soothing sounds. If she didn't complain, I'd rave about Jeff's mother's choices. If she got flustered over any decisions she might be allowed to make, I'd hug her and assure her every bride found planning her wedding overwhelming. To keep the rules fresh in my mind, the next time I went to the store, I'd buy giant-sized sticky notes, write on them my rules for Marie's wedding, and stick them beside those with Della's admonition to never say "I told you so."

I crunched a piece of ice from my glass of tea. "I'll have a bridal shower for you," I said, trying to sound thrilled. There was no way I could not invite Jeff's mother. "Do you have a preference for a theme?"

"Kitchen, I think. No one ever has enough kitchen gadgets."

"Great. I'll ask everyone to include a favorite recipe."

"I love you, Honey," she said. "I know how much you hate showers." Marie giggled. "I'll never forget the bridal shower for June Miller. You looked so grim I giggled every time I looked at you."

"The sweetness of the punch made my teeth ache, and June's shrieking over every gift she opened made my head ache."

Marie's wedding would be a disaster for me.

By the time Marie left to drive home, the muscles of my face hurt from being forced into a happy expression. The minute she was out of sight, I let my lips turn down, my eyelids droop, and my cheeks sag. There are some things one could not be joyful about.

When Della got back, she took one look at me and shook her head. I told her about Marie's wedding plans and about Jeff's mother.

"You'll get through this, Honey. And you'll be a better person for it."

"Jeff's mother is a control freak who will make Marie's life difficult long after the wedding."

"Even if your in-laws are wonderful people, it isn't easy," Della said.

"Marie promised I could choose the attendants' dresses. But I'm sure Jeff's mother will have the final say, and I'll end up wearing a dress that makes me look like a whale. I can only hope the color isn't puce. Brownish-purple makes me look green."

"Speaking of green," Della said, "I need to get to the grocery store before it closes. Anything you want or need?"

"Some ginger tea."

"Okay. I should be back in an hour."

I fixed some iced ginger tea from the last two bags and spent the rest of the evening sitting on the beach sipping cold tea while Bowser kept busy examining anything interesting he came across.

The next afternoon, I took Bowser with me and showed up at Sam's for our scheduled practice time. Ace was sitting at a table outside of Sam's. The minute he saw us, he smiled and waved. Yesterday's moodiness was no longer evident.

In the practice room, Bowser watched from the sidelines as Ace and I worked on the advanced steps we were adding to our basic routine. After an hour and a half, we started collecting our things before leaving.

Ace replaced his second dance shoe with a flip-flop. "Emily and I had dinner at a great place the other night."

My heart froze. "Where?"

"In New Bernwick. There's a competition there this Saturday. I signed us up."

I narrowed my eyes. "Okay. But next time I'd appreciate it if you checked with me first. I might have a date—"

"With who?" He sounded skeptical.

"With someone."

I was mad over his signing us up without asking me. I was mad over my lack of willpower to say, "Sorry, I can't make it this Saturday." I called to Bowser and rushed us out the exit door. Instead of taking the lead, Bowser trotted alongside me. Feeling tender and vulnerable, I appreciated his sensing my mood and staying beside me.

I strolled down the beach toward the B and B, my head down and my hands stuffed in the pockets of my capri pants. I kept moving forward, concentrating my mind on the patterns the wind and water had sculpted in the sand.

Bowser barked. I looked up. He set off toward a gull, sending it into flight. He ran back and then passed me going in the opposite direction. I should have had enough sense to put him on his leash to keep him from going his own way. But I was all out of good sense.

I turned to call him back.

Ace was coming up the beach with Bowser trotting beside him.

I wasn't about to surrender Bowser to Ace. I waited for them.

"Hey, Honey," Ace said. "You left before I could tell you—"

"I have something to do."

He ignored my curt remark. "Della called earlier. She wants to talk to me about the goats. Since I'm going to the B and B, I thought I'd walk back with you."

"Come along, Bowser," I said in a commanding voice and

resumed walking as fast as I could toward the B and B. Ace kept up. Bowser took the middle position. I think Ace had no idea what I was upset about. But I didn't owe him an explanation of my emotions. And he wasn't exactly radiating joy either. Only Bowser trotting along between us appeared happy.

"Shall I cancel Saturday?" he asked. "Betty and Sam will be there."

I didn't answer. Bowser, Ace, and I continued around to the street side. Inside the front door, I picked up Bowser and started up the stairs. "What time should I be ready?"

"Five."

Ace went into Della's office. A good twenty minutes later, when I came down to get something to drink, Ace and Della were sitting at the kitchen table.

"Hey, Honey," Della said. "Sit down. I've got great news."

Now what? I poured a glass of sweet tea, found a slice of lemon, and squeezed the juice into my glass. I sat down. Ace and Della grinned at me.

"They've caught the arsonist, and it isn't Ace?" I said without smiling.

Della frowned at me. "No."

I turned my head to look at Ace and raised my eyebrows. "Then what?"

Della beamed like a schoolgirl who'd won the spelling bee. "Emily and Ace are buying the goat farm."

I took a large sip of my tea and swallowed. A lemon seed headed for my windpipe. I managed to stop its progress and then spit the seed into my hand before it could do any damage.

"Why are you selling the farm?" I asked, trying to sound neutral about the issue.

"Harry asked me to go to Florida with him. I said I would."

"What?" I half rose out of my chair. My hand knocked over my glass of tea. I got myself into a full upright position. Ace was up and tearing sheets off the paper towel roll. He started mopping up the table.

"Sorry I startled you, Honey," Della said and boomed a laugh. "But sit down. There's more."

More? My knees were as shaky as a half-set dish of Jell-O. I dropped back onto the chair seat.

Ace finished mopping up the tea and tossed the soggy towels in the trash.

Della covered my hand with hers. "Before I put the B and B on the market, I'm offering you the opportunity to buy it with no down payment, and I'll hold the mortgage. We can work out a payment schedule so during the season the payments will be bigger and during the off-season substantially less."

My entire body froze—nothing would move, not even my eyelids.

Della took my hand and squeezed hard. "There's no penalty, Honey. If it doesn't work out, I can always put it on the market later."

"Why is Harry going to Florida?" I squeaked.

"He's taking a job as a captain for a luxury yacht charter company. An old friend recommended him. He interviewed with the owner two weeks ago, and they offered him a job. I'm hiring on as part of his crew."

"Have you ever sailed anything bigger than a Sunfish?" I asked.

"I'm hiring on as cook, Honey."

"Once you're under sail, you can't get off, you know. You'll be Harry's captive. And what about keeping your independence, running your own business, and not having to answer to anyone?"

"The farm and the B and B have been great, but they tie me down. I'm getting out of my rut, heading for a new adventure and facing a new challenge before I'm too old."

"Sounds good to me," Ace said, sitting down again.

Okay. I could understand this. I know something about being stuck in a rut. And Della's face and expression were younger and happier than I'd seen her look in years.

"Can I take a day or two to think before I give you my answer?"

I couldn't believe what I'd just said. I had a life and a job that I loved miles away from here. And running a B and B full time would push me far beyond my comfort zone.

Della let go of my hand. "Sure, think about it until the morning and then let me know what you want to do."

Ace having signed up for a competition without asking me first, and then Della giving me one night to decide about making a major change in my life, created a lot of anxiety.

I chewed on my bottom lip.

"If you do buy the B and B, Honey, I'll be around to help," Ace said. "Emily's hired a couple of part-time workers. She can run the farm pretty much on her own."

I turned toward Ace and stared right into his eyes. "Thanks, but if I buy the B and B, I won't need a handyman." I smiled— hoping it didn't look as fake as it felt. "I can relight pilot lights and unstop toilets."

At least after Marie taught me how, I could.

I wasn't handling my accelerating emotional turmoil well at the moment—evidenced by the increase in the rate of my eye blinking.

Ace got up from the table. "Emily and I are buying a new milk machine tonight." He didn't glance at me. "Practice tomorrow, Honey?"

"Okay." Having agreed to go with him on Saturday, I couldn't avoid practice. It wasn't in me to not work at being the best I could be.

Ace called good-bye and hurried out of the kitchen.

Della went to the refrigerator and began taking out the ingredients for supper.

I picked another seed out of my glass. Bowser had bonded with Ace. Ace had bonded with Emily. Marie had bonded with Jeff, Della had bonded with Harry. I had Bowser—part of the time.

Della sounded a sparkling laugh. "Things work out funny sometimes, Honey."

"Do they? I'm going to spend some time with Bowser before we eat."

In my case, the saying that the older one gets, the wiser one gets didn't seem true. However, all was not yet lost. As Ace and I made our way around the shag dance circuit, I could meet a single man or even two whose passion for shag dancing matched mine—a male who I'd want to pursue at the end of my sabbatical. I'd keep my eyes open and my expectations high.

But before I could worry about anything else, I had to make a decision about the dilemma Della had tossed at me. She needed a quick answer. I needed some time to sort out how I wanted to answer. I sat on the floor next to Bowser and considered what running the B and B on my own would involve.

There wasn't much business in October. Della closed in November and then opened up in April. I could hire someone to run the place on the weekdays when I'd be teaching.

I let Bowser out. When he came in, I set up the gate and let him stay in the parlor while I went to see if there was anything left I could do to help Della with supper.

After we ate, I went to my room and started a list of the pros and cons of buying the B and B. It'd be hard, but with good help, I could manage teaching and running the B and B. Millie was due back from Europe at the end of August. She'd worked for Della for ten years. Maybe she'd be interested in living in and taking over the weekday management.

In the early spring and late fall, most of the guests were weekends only. And in the months when the B and B was booked full seven days a week, as soon as school ended, I could be here full time. I put this on the pro side.

On the con side, I added what became my deciding factor. If Della sold both the B and B and the goat farm, and working for Harry didn't go well, she'd have no business to return to. So, instead of buying it, I'd offer to keep it open for a year and see how it went. By the end of a year, Della should know if life on the high seas and if not being her own boss suited her, and I'd know if I wanted to own a B and B.

The next morning I was up so early, I got to the kitchen before Della. I started the coffee and set out the juice.

Della shuffled in, yawned, and poured herself a cup of coffee. I joined her at the table.

"I have my answer."

She perked up. "And?"

"I'm not committing to buying the place, but I'll run it for a year and then, if you still want to sell, I should know if I want to buy it."

Della gave me a big grin. "Thanks, Honey. Harry and I have to leave by the end of this week."

I wasn't going to say a negative word to Della about her harebrained scheme. I didn't want my doubts about how happy she'd be working for Harry to topple the gilt-edged cloud she was sailing on at the moment.

I added a second spoonful of sugar to my coffee. In a week, the full responsibility for this place would be mine.

Della shoved back her chair and pulled out the frying pan

from the drawer beneath the oven. "I'll ask Polly Wilcock to come in to help you. She's filled in for Millie before, so she knows the routine."

"Great."

"And don't hesitate to ask Ace for help."

"I won't."

The last thing I'd do was ask Ace for help. I'd buy an instruction book on home repairs. If I couldn't fix something, I'd call Marie. If she couldn't help me over the phone, I'd hire a licensed electrician or plumber or whatever trade would be required to fix the problem. And I'd ask Della to give me the secret to her pecan rolls before she left.

"I'll be fine. I'm happy for you. Change is good. And don't spend a second during your new adventure worrying about me," I said. And I wasn't going to worry about Della suffocating under Harry's command and chafing at living in close quarters with a crew and dealing with people who chartered boats—at least I'd try not to.

The list of things I wasn't allowing myself to worry about or express my concerns over was getting pretty long. But if I could remain joyful and optimistic at least three-quarters of the time, all my worrying should get balanced out.

When I showed up for dance practice the next afternoon, I told Ace about the arrangement I'd made with Della.

"Good luck," he said and didn't add anything more.

Our practice went great. We could now read each other so well that Ace could change our routine with a quick flick of his eyes. More important, he didn't say or do anything more to upset me or make it hard for me to keep a safe emotional distance from him. For my part, I kept my conversation brief and my facial expressions friendly but sober.

I caught him staring at me a couple of times with a puzzled

look in his eyes. I'd be happy to tell him my perfectly good reasons for icing our relationship, but if I did, I'd be exposing my vulnerabilities.

On Saturday, we placed second. Betty and Sam took first again.

Ace said he was happy. I said I was happy too, but I'd be happier when we came in first.

So far, Ace had been doing the advanced steps while I kept to the basic step most of the time. I'd noticed the other couples mirrored their advanced steps more often than not. Halfway home, my competitive drive loosened up my planned distancing behavior.

"If we're serious about trying for Nationals, we'll need to up our degree of difficulty even more. I'll practice mirroring you on the boogie walk. See how it goes."

He glanced over at me and smiled his heartwarming smile— the smile that made it impossible for me to keep my temperature from overheating.

He tapped the wheel with the palm of his hand. "I think you're right. If it's okay, I'll ask Emily to come to our practice on Monday and videotape us. We can study the tape and see where we need to improve."

"Sure. Good idea." I drew back into myself. I didn't want to like Emily, but she was friendly and outgoing and unpretentious, which made my disliking her difficult.

On Monday, Emily showed up at Sam's back room with a video camera. The tape of our routine was revealing. On a couple of occasions, our arms dropped too low. There were times when one or the other of us messed up on our footwork. Besides increasing the difficulty of our steps, we concentrated on improving our posture, keeping our handhold loose, and maintaining a smooth glide.

The next competition we entered, Ace and I took first against many of the top competitors we'd faced before, including Sam and Betty. Our hard work had paid off.

On the way home, Ace pulled into the parking lot of a café. Other than the man working behind the counter, we were alone.

We both ordered the blue-plate special, chicken-fried steak with mashed potatoes and kale. The food tasted terrific.

The counterman came over, refilled our coffee cups, and took away our empty plates.

Ace looked at me across the table. His eyes were pools of happiness. "We did it, Honey. We won."

I looked at the tabletop and stirred my coffee. "We did. It's been fun, Ace." I raised my eyes and looked at him. "But I can't continue dancing with you."

His eyes clouded with disbelief. He leaned back in the seat—putting as much space in the confined booth between us as he could. "Why?"

"Because I'll be too busy running the B and B. I'll have to learn how to do the paperwork, plus the cleaning, and fixing breakfast every day. And I'm determined to do whatever I need to support Marie through the pitfalls of planning her wedding. I won't have any time left for practice or for competitions."

Ace took a long sip of his coffee. He set the cup down and pursed his lips. "Okay. I understand. Taking on the B and B is a big job on top of everything else you've committed to."

"It is. Shag dancing with you has been great, but I can't do everything, and it's important to me to keep the business going in case Della decides to come back."

Ace slid out of the booth and offered me his hand. I took it and slid out of my side to join him. He paid the counterman.

In the car, I got up the courage to ask him if Emily shag danced.

"No," he said.

Relief washed over me. At least Emily wouldn't be taking my place as Ace's partner on the dance floor.

We didn't talk much for the remainder of the ride home, but the atmosphere inside the car wasn't tense.

At the B and B, Ace pulled up as close to the porch steps as he could. He didn't turn off the engine. " 'Night, Honey."

" 'Night, Ace." I opened the door and got out. By the time I had my foot on the first porch step, his car was at the end of the driveway. I knew he was disappointed over the ending of our partnership. So was I, but as much as I loved shag dancing and competing, my time and energy would be taken up by more important things.

At least until Marie's wedding was over, and I knew Della's adventure was working out and she wasn't coming back.

Chapter Nine

The going-away party for Della and Harry was held at the community center the night before they were leaving. It didn't end until well past one.

When my alarm clock buzzed the next morning, I'd turned it off and fallen back asleep. Della was so busy saying good-bye to all the people who showed up to watch her and Harry drive off, it was 6:45 before she noticed and came up to wake me.

She gave me a big hug and said to set out cold things for the guests for breakfast and not to worry about serving anything hot.

I splashed water on my face, brushed my teeth, made a quick swipe at my unruly morning hair, and put on a pair of shorts and T-shirt straight out of the clean-clothes basket.

I got downstairs just in time to wave good-bye to Della and Harry as they went down the driveway in Harry's SUV, with every inch of the SUV's interior except for the driver and passenger seats packed full with their gear. Anything they couldn't fit in the car, they'd sold or donated to charity.

I stood in the B and B kitchen and wiped away my tears.

I didn't have time to cry or worry. I had fifteen guests who would start showing up for breakfast in an hour.

I got the coffee brewing and the orange and grapefruit juice set out.

"Hey, Honey."

I ignored the speaker, but my panic quieted.

"What can I help with?" Ace asked.

I glanced in his direction out of the corner of my eye.

He was leaning against the doorframe again.

"Thanks, but I'm keeping breakfast simple today."

I straightened up, keeping my back to him, and headed for the pantry door.

Ace would be a big help. But having him around would make it too hard to keep a damper on my feelings for him. He'd kept his word and hadn't tried to kiss me again or even hold my hand. Not even the night we beat Betty and Sam. But my memory of his kiss still gave me shivers.

"Thanks for offering to help," I called as I retreated. "You don't need to stay. I've got everything under control." I shouted the last sentence from the doorway of the walk-in pantry. I picked up a box of oat cereal and waited several seconds. *Make him go away.* I took a deep breath. *Please.*

When I came out of the pantry, Ace was leaning against the kitchen counter. The look in his eyes resembled that of a courtroom prosecutor about to destroy the testimony of a hapless defense witness.

My heart twanged like the strings of a bluegrass fiddle.

"You look frazzled, Honey." He pushed away from the counter and went to the refrigerator and took out two packages of sausage.

I smoothed back my hair with the palm of my hand.

"Bowser wasn't cooperative this morning," I said. "I got behind on the time."

I collected place mats and utensils and went into the breakfast room to set up the tables.

The smell of sausage browning made my eyes water. I went upstairs, splashed cold water on my face, put on a light coat of lipstick, and got my hair corralled into a neat ponytail.

By the time I returned to the kitchen, Ace was whistling a jaunty tune, cracking eggs, and dumping the contents into a large bowl. "French toast," he said.

People who take over when they haven't been asked shouldn't be allowed to get away with their passive-aggressive behavior. I considered arming myself with a cast-iron frying pan and commanding him to leave and never return.

But this morning I needed help.

Because I didn't want him to get the impression I liked him being here, I answered either yes or no to his questions.

I filled a pitcher with cream and then filled the sugar bowl.

By the time I'd gotten a speech composed to impress on Ace that he wasn't welcome in the future, guests could be heard in the breakfast room. I went out to greet them.

Ace stayed until the dishes were done and put away. He was a good man to have around in the mornings. It was nice to have the energy of another body nearby. But it'd be better if the other body in the kitchen weren't Ace.

He wiped off the kitchen table and tossed the dishcloth into the sink. "I'm taking you to lunch today. Be ready at twelve thirty."

Clear and direct. I took it for granted we'd be visiting Miss Crandell and Hattie for lunch—which was fine. And his easy manner had mellowed out my resistance a bit. "Okay. Thanks for the help this morning."

So much for my intention to put my foot down and insist he not darken the door of the B and B again unless invited.

Ace said good-bye.

Polly couldn't start work until tomorrow, so all the cleaning for today would be my responsibility.

Fueled by exasperation over my letting Ace have his way again, I got each guest room cleaned in record time.

I took Bowser for a walk and then had a long shower. I put on a pair of capri pants and a top I'd ironed. I added mascara to my lashes. By 12:25, Bowser and I were ready and sitting on the porch waiting for Ace to show up.

When he arrived, he sauntered toward the porch in the eye-catching, breathtaking way he had. He was whistling the same jaunty tune he'd been whistling in the kitchen this morning—a tune far too lively for shag dancing.

"Your lordship," he said with a nod to Bowser, who'd risen up on his hind legs to greet him. "Sorry, my man, you won't be coming with us this time. You're assigned watch duty at the B and B."

"Won't Miss Crandell be upset if Bowser doesn't come too?" I asked.

Ace looked at me for a long second. "She would, but we aren't going to Miss Crandell's."

"Oh. Well, maybe I won't—"

"Honey, we're going to lunch. It's important."

"Where?"

"Siler's."

"You want to tell me what's so important I have to surrender my right to object?"

"No."

I hesitated for several seconds and then gave in again—because I was curious, because I wanted to, because I had no backbone.

I stashed Bowser in our room. He looked crestfallen. "I know, boy." I leaned down and scratched his head. "But you're a member of the Resistance and Ace is your commander." I sounded silly, but it didn't stop me. "You have to follow orders. When I get back, I'll let you frolic on the beach for a long time. Tomorrow I promise to take you for a visit with Miss Crandell and Hattie."

And I promised myself that from now on, I'd say what I wanted in a clear and direct way.

Ace drove to Siler's without speaking.

Inside the restaurant, he guided me to a table in the back.

We ordered. And then Ace looked at me, his gaze fixed on me and serious.

"Okay, Honey, tell me what's wrong."

I closed my eyes. Eyes give things away.

"What makes you think something's wrong?"

"You're closed down. You've stopped talking about anything other than the practical details of whatever is happening at the moment."

I began folding and unfolding a paper napkin. "I don't like burdening other people with my worries, Ace. The truth is, I worry about too many things I can't do much about."

"Like?"

"Like Marie's future mother-in-law making trouble. As sweet as Marie is, I don't think being bossed around by her mother-in-law will make her happy."

"Doesn't she know her future mother-in-law is controlling?"

"She does, but I think she's in denial about what it will mean to her future."

"What else?"

Ace's soft voice and caring eyes compelled me to share.

"I agreed to take over the B and B because I didn't want Della to have no place to return to if she changes her mind. And I don't know how I'm going to do it all once school starts."

Ace reached over and placed his hand on my arm. "I doubt Della will change her mind. She and Harry have been together a long time. She wouldn't be happy here without Harry."

"But Harry might change his mind, and they could both come back."

Ace removed his hand and sat back in the chair. His eyes stayed focused on me. His expression was both tender and intense. He pursed his lips. "I'm willing to help out at the B and B. Emily's got things at the farm under control. My only job there is to take care of any legal work and then help if she needs me."

"So you have time on your hands?" I managed a weak smile.

Ace gave a tension-breaking laugh. "Yup. And if I don't find something to fill my idle time with, I'm likely to get in trouble." Ace grinned. "Which would get me in trouble with Miss Crandell and Hattie."

I picked up a potato chip from my plate and broke it in half. What would be worse, seeing Ace or not seeing Ace? At least if I saw him, I'd know what he was doing and wouldn't have to fish for information about him from Miss Crandell and Hattie.

"If you promise to stop doing things like signing me up for competitions and taking me to lunch without asking if I can or want to go, I'll consider hiring you as the chief pecan roll maker and general kitchen help."

"Will it be good enough to say I'll try to remember to ask?"

I looked up at the ceiling, considering. I had to know if he was serious or teasing. I looked into his eyes. He didn't look like he was teasing. "Okay, but if you forget and I say no, you have to promise you won't try to change my mind."

"It's a deal. Have you considered maybe I don't ask because I'm afraid you'll say no?"

Oh. My. Gosh. I had to change this conversation and fast before I lost total control of my heart.

I sat back and forced a smile. "By the way, I know your real first name and it isn't Ace."

He leaned forward, raised his eyebrows, and narrowed his eyes. "Who ratted?"

"Miss Crandell. But not on purpose. She referred to you as Wallace once."

"Wallace Sanford's my lawyer name."

"Impressive."

"Ace Sanford's my handyman name."

We both laughed, which released the tension between us.

But I knew I was on wobbly ground. Ace cared enough to ask what was bothering me and to listen to my woes. He cared enough to promise he'd try to stop expecting me to go along with his plans. And he worried about my saying no.

Ace swallowed the last of his turkey club sandwich. "I not only like being with you because we dance well together, I like being with you because you're caring and sensitive and cute."

I could wrap dreams around those words. I'm pretty sure I radiated joy. I looked up at Ace. And then, to cover my out-of-control emotions, I laughed Della's booming laugh. It steadied my nerves.

"Thanks," I said. "You told me once you think goats are cute." My voice sounded nice and steady.

"They are."

"Hmm. Eye of the beholder."

He chuckled.

But I'd been watching, and I hadn't seen a hint of amusement in his eyes when he said he liked being with me and he thought I was cute.

By the time we left the restaurant, I felt better about everything working out okay at the B and B. With Ace's help, getting breakfast together would be faster and easier. If Ace and Emily paired up, I'd get the rip in my heart patched and get on with my life. I had two jobs I loved, a great dog, and super friends—everything one needed to enjoy life. Having a man I loved would be nice too, but I'd be okay if it didn't happen.

On our drive from the restaurant to the B and B, I mentioned having promised Bowser I'd take him to the beach to compensate for his being left at home.

Ace parked. He got out of the car and went around the house while I went inside to get Bowser. Maybe there was something he wanted to check on. Or was he planning to join Bowser and me even if I hadn't invited him? On the other hand, maybe I'd mentioned taking Bowser for a walk hoping Ace would join us. And maybe if I learned to say what I wanted in a more direct way, I wouldn't have to work so hard to get it.

Bowser saw Ace under the deck and ran over to greet him.

"You want to walk with us?" I called. Very direct.

Ace emerged from the open space below the deck. "Thanks, I was hoping you'd ask." He smiled a smile as bright as Marie's diamond.

The waves weren't very big, but a couple of surfers were out in the water. A shrimp boat with its nets raised sailed northward, headed back to its dock. I picked up an unbroken half shell and turned it over in my hand. "How come you don't work at your law practice much?"

"Because I hate being indoors. I have a couple of clients— real estate investors—who keep me on retainer. It earns me enough to eat and pay the rent."

"When did you start doing odd jobs for Della?"

Ace shoved his fingers into the pockets of his shorts. "Harry and I grew up together. When I came back here, I started fishing with him on weekends. When Hurricane Bob turned and headed straight for us, Harry had to get his boat out of here. I helped Della put up the hurricane shutters, clear up around the house, and evacuate. She and I became friends." Ace bent down and gave Bowser a head scratch. "Thanks for the walk. I'm going to jog back to the B and B to get my car. I'll see you in the morning."

I stashed Bowser in our room and then went to the grocery store and bought a ten-pound bag of flour and five pounds of pecans. In the morning, I'd ask Ace to make the dough for the pecan rolls.

Della was right. Ace was a good guy. And having him as my friend and—if he'd wait until I had the time to practice and compete again—my shag dance partner, I'd be happy.

Chapter Ten

I'd set my alarm clock for fifteen minutes earlier so I could shower and comb my hair, curl my eyelashes, and put on mascara.

As I came down the stairs to let Bowser out, I could smell coffee brewing. By the time I got Bowser settled and entered the breakfast room, the cold cereals and the juice were set out.

"Hey," Ace said when he spotted me in the doorway.

"Hey." My attitude toward him had spun a 180-degree turn from yesterday morning. Instead of being provoked over his being in my kitchen, I was happy he was here.

We worked together in the kitchen with the same awareness of each other's moves as we had on the dance floor.

We were filling plates when Polly showed up for her first day of helping me clean the rooms.

Ace stayed until the kitchen was clean and tidy again. But he left before I'd remembered to ask him to make the dough for Della's pecan rolls. I'd try making the dough later in the day. If it didn't turn out, I'd ask Ace to do it tomorrow.

I pushed the vacuum cleaner around the parlor. My stress

level had descended to a range I could handle. The guests had complimented the breakfast, and with Polly helping clean the rooms, the physical work should be done before noon, leaving me free to work in the office.

But with Della gone, the place felt lonely.

As soon as I got everything in order, I called Marie and invited her to come and stay for a few days. It'd be great having her here; she'd help with breakfast, and I'd have a short respite from seeing Ace every morning.

She said she'd let me know by tomorrow.

The next day, I was working on the accounts in the office when someone tapped on the doorframe. I turned. Marie stood there with a big smile on her face.

"Oh, my gosh. I'm so glad to see you." I jumped up to hug her. My eyes filled with tears.

"Hey, Honey. The minute I finished talking to you yesterday, I started packing and then I got all the things on my current 'to do' list crossed out so I could come today," Marie said.

"You should have called back to tell me."

Marie burst into tears.

I patted her back and let her cry for a few minutes, positive the strain of getting ready for her wedding was the cause of her tears.

"Go upstairs and wash your face. I'll fill two glasses with tea. We can sit on the deck."

She swiped at the tear trails on her cheeks. "Thanks, Honey." She sounded as woeful as she looked. She turned and then went up the stairs dragging her suitcase behind her.

When she came out to the deck the tears were gone, but her expression told me I should keep quiet and wait for her to speak. And when she did I'd listen, be supportive, say nothing bad about Jeff, about his mother, or about the wedding plans.

I stretched out in the lounge chair and picked up my glass of tea.

We sat there for a long time. Neither of us spoke. I started to doze off.

"Honey?" Marie's voice was not much louder than a whisper.

"Hmm."

"I'm not getting married."

"Okay."

"Jeff wasn't exaggerating about his mother being bossy."

"Hmm."

"I asked him to move with me to California so we could be on our own. He got angry and said he wasn't moving anywhere."

I sat up. "Are you moving to California?"

"No. But I had to know how attached Jeff was to his family."

"Very, I'd guess."

"I'd always come second," Marie said and fished a piece of ice from her glass of tea.

"So, what now?"

"I'm keeping my job, at least for next year, and then I'll decide what I want to do."

"I'd love it if you'd spend the rest of the summer here."

"Thanks. You're a great friend, Honey. I think you knew Jeff's mother would be trouble, but you kept it to yourself."

Marie wouldn't have listened if I'd told her. But I wasn't going to say a word about the strong misgivings I had about her marriage in the first place—and not only because of his mother. Things could change again and she'd end up married to Jeff after all. And if she did, I didn't want to have said or done anything that would end our friendship because sooner or later Marie might need a friend she could trust.

"Love's a funny thing, Marie." I downed half my glass of tea.

She nodded her agreement. "So, how are things going with you?" she asked.

"Pretty good. I hired a person Della recommended to help clean the rooms. She's great. Ace has been coming by in the morning to help with breakfast."

"Wow. How's Ace look early in the morning?"

I laughed. "Shaved and showered. But, best of all, he's a good cook."

"Do the two of you have anything going on other than being dance partners?"

"You know I'm on sabbatical."

"And two days ago, I was engaged to be married."

I pointed to the brown pelicans dive-bombing the ocean to scoop up their dinner.

We watched them for a while.

"Life is a series of surprises," I said.

"And shocks," Marie added.

"Let's walk down to Primms for dinner," I said.

"I'd like to."

We cleaned up and headed for Primms.

We asked for a table on Primms' outdoor verandah and then ordered fresh-caught, steamed shrimp. We talked about school and laughed again at some of the funny moments from last year. By the time we got back to the B and B, I felt truly joyful. With Marie's wedding called off, I could stop worrying about her long-term happiness. I could let go of my dread over the thought of wearing an awful dress and standing around at her wedding reception trying to look happy. Best of all, I wouldn't have to throw a shower for her.

And with Marie staying here, the place would no longer be lonely.

Marie was up early. She and Ace greeted each other and discussed goats for a while. I put her to work filling the cereal containers.

Ace tended to a griddle full of Della's homemade sausage links. "You picked out your wedding dress yet?" he asked Marie.

Marie gave a tiny sob and burst into tears.

I should have told Ace that Marie's wedding was off.

"Sit at the table, Marie. Tell Ace what happened. I'll get a box of tissues."

Ace pulled out a chair for Marie and gave her a hug. When I got back with the tissues, Ace was sitting across from Marie with his elbows propped on the table and his chin resting atop his bridged fingers. He was giving her his full attention. Marie gazed at the tabletop while telling Ace about her confrontation with Jeff's mother. Details she hadn't even shared with me. I caught the tail end of a sentence.

". . . And then his mother said my dress had too much yellow in the fabric and too much material through the hips. She said it made me look sallow and chubby."

Ace looked at me and rolled his eyes. "A bully never changes, Marie. It's good you stood up for yourself before it was too late."

Ace pushed away from the table. He moved the sausage links from the griddle to a foil-lined tray and put the tray in the oven. "I'm turning off the oven. The sausages will be fine. The two of you can finish the breakfast," he said.

I suppose with Marie here, he could trust me to handle breakfast. I was beginning to think the real reason he showed up here in the mornings was because he felt an obligation to Della to make sure I didn't ruin the business she'd worked so hard to build.

I diced up a fresh melon and added the chunks to the bowl of assorted fruit. Ace had said he liked being here, he'd said he liked being with me, but the minute someone else was around to help, he took off.

Which was fine.

Marie's a great cook and she can fix things. Keeping her

busy would be good for her, and having her here would be good for me.

As soon as the guests had been fed, and Polly went off to clean the rooms, Marie and I got the kitchen cleaned up. When all was neat and tidy, Marie asked if she could take Bowser for a walk. I said he'd be grateful. Bowser is good company. He'd keep Marie's mind off Jeff.

I went to help Polly.

When Marie and Bowser returned, I gave Bowser a thorough brushing. A visit to Miss Crandell and Hattie would do all of us good.

Miss Crandell and Hattie greeted us with the delight they always showed whenever I visited. Miss Crandell cradled Bowser in her lap while Hattie served up her cold lemonade and benne seed cookies.

Our hostesses both gave Marie their sympathetic attention while she told them the reasons she'd called off her wedding. Every now and then Hattie would mutter, "Well, I declare," and Miss Crandell would cluck her tongue.

Marie blew her nose. "And that's when I told Jeff the wedding was off and I never wanted to see him again," she concluded.

"You did right, Miss Marie," Hattie said and passed the plate of cookies for the third time.

Miss Crandell sat up with an expression on her face I'd seen before when she'd been incensed over something. "Coming eye to eye with a shark is not as scary as dealing with some mothers-in-law. I've heard way too many stories over the years about a mother-in-law being unkind to a daughter-in-law, but I do believe your story is the worst I ever heard."

Marie sniffed. "Thank you, Miss Crandell. I was beginning to think I was too sensitive, or with everything his mother had to do to pull off the wedding of the year, her nerves were strained."

"Strained nerves are no excuse for being cruel."

Bowser jumped down from Miss Crandell's lap. He climbed into Marie's lap and licked her face. Marie snuggled him to her.

"You're right, Bowser. What I need is a dog," Marie said.

We all nodded in agreement.

Marie and I said good-bye. Miss Crandell and Hattie told us to come back anytime, as they always did and they always meant. I bent down to kiss Miss Crandell's soft downy cheek. She squeezed my hand. "Everything's going to work out like it's supposed to. You just wait and see," she said. "And the next time you see Ace, tell him to come see me."

I was surprised when Ace showed up the next morning. Marie wasn't up, and I didn't want to wake her. I'd planned to keep breakfast simple. I hadn't gotten around to attempting the yeast dough for the pecan rolls, but I didn't want to have to rely on Ace to make them. Until I mastered the pecan rolls, I'd serve my streusel coffee cake.

Ace and I went about our routine in the same efficient way we had every morning.

He stood at the counter grating a big block of cheddar cheese.

"I've invited Marie to stay for the rest of the summer," I said. "She's a great cook, and she can fix things." I cut cubes of butter into brown sugar for the streusel topping. "With Marie here, I won't need you to help me out."

Marie hadn't said she was staying, but I was pretty sure she would. I told Ace about the visit Marie and I had with Miss Crandell and Hattie and how Marie felt better after the visit.

Ace put the grater in the sink and leaned back against the counter. "Spending the summer here would be good for Marie."

"I think so too." I looked over at him. "Miss Crandell asked me to tell you she wants you to come see her."

He stopped me as I started past him on my way to get a carton of eggs from the refrigerator. "Why do you suppose Miss Crandell asked you to pass on her message?"

"I—" I stood there mute and frozen by the intensity in his eyes. Something powerful enough to take my breath away zinged between us. I didn't know what to name it. "I have no idea."

I managed to continue past him. The blast of cold from the open refrigerator cooled my face and brought me back to my senses. I grabbed the egg carton and the plastic container of milk and set them on the counter.

"I'm gone, Honey," Ace said.

"Be back here at twelve. We're going to lunch," I said in my schoolteacher voice.

"Are you asking me?"

I turned and smiled. "I'm telling you."

He curled his lips together and then grinned. "Payback, huh?" He spun around and disappeared before I could draw in a deep breath.

I was proud of myself for having said what I wanted in a clear and direct way. If he showed up for lunch, I hoped to have the courage to say what I needed to say.

The smell of grits burning sent me rushing to the stove. I snatched the smoking pan off the burner and set it in the sink.

"What's that awful smell?" Marie stood in the doorway waving her hand in front of her nose.

"Burned grits."

She hurried across the kitchen to the sliding door and opened it. "I'll start a fresh batch," she said. "Are you okay? You don't look so good."

"I'm fine. I'm taking Ace to lunch today."

"What's the occasion?"

"A frank talk with him."

She found a clean pan and filled a measuring cup with water. "About?"

"I'll tell you later. After I see how it goes. See if I have the courage to say what I want to say."

"Which is?"

"He needs to name his emotions. He doesn't have to rescue me, and he can stop worrying Della's star rating will drop if he doesn't show up to make sure the breakfast gets raves, and he shouldn't be upset with Miss Crandell and Hattie."

"Maybe Della's star rating isn't why he shows up every morning." Marie measured out the correct amount of water, dumped it in the pan, and turned on the burner.

"What other reason could he have? Except for our being dance partners, we don't have a relationship."

Marie was stirring the grits to prevent lumps. "Maybe you don't want to see that he likes you."

"He kissed me once for real, but it was because he got carried away over having a shag dance partner he could win with. Since then, unless we're dancing, he hasn't even tried to hold my hand."

"I'm betting you scared him off."

"I think he's scared of having his sore spots exposed. He got upset this morning when I told him Miss Crandell asked me to tell him she wanted him to visit."

"Why?"

"I can't imagine. Maybe she's been pestering him about me. She and Hattie are scheming about something. I'm pretty sure Ace and Emily are dating. He mentioned taking her to dinner."

"And?"

"He got upset when I told him I wouldn't need him here because you could cook and do repairs."

"Honey, you know better than to say things that wound a man's ego. And I didn't say I'd be here."

"You aren't going to stay?"

"I am. It's beautiful, and peaceful, and I'll have something to do besides sit around feeling sorry for myself."

"Oh, Marie, I'm so glad. After Della left, this place got superquiet at night."

"We make a good team, Honey."

I gave her a big hug. "We make a super team."

I'd planned on packing a lunch so Ace and I could eat in the park where there'd be no chance our conversation could be overheard.

When I opened the bread box, except for a flattened commercial bakery wrapper containing two heels, it was empty.

The deli up the road made great sandwiches. I got Bowser and my purse.

Bowser chose to walk in the grass. His head drooped. He showed no interest in exploring any of the objects along our route. I didn't think he looked so forlorn because he sensed my anxiety. I think he knew Ace had been at the B and B this morning and he didn't get to see him.

I tied Bowser's leash around a pole outside the deli.

While the two turkey subs I'd ordered were being put together, I eyed the dessert case.

I didn't buy dessert.

With the lump in my throat, I didn't know if I'd be able to eat much of anything.

Back at the B and B, I found a small cooler for the sandwiches and fixed a thermos of sweet tea.

At five to twelve, I collected the picnic things and went out to the porch to wait for Ace.

Ten minutes later, I began pacing.

At seven after, his car turned into the driveway. He pulled into a parking spot and cut the engine. He was talking on a cell phone.

He motioned for me to come over.

I opened the car door and put the cooler on the floor.

"That's great news. Thanks for letting me know," he said.

Ace ended the call. "You'll never guess."

"Probably not," I said, hoping I sounded normal.

"They've arrested the arsonist."

"Who?"

"Charley Henley's son, Mike. The kid's fourteen. His dad brought him in to the sheriff's office this morning and he confessed. He'll be tried in juvenile court. I hope he'll get straightened out."

"It's sad. I hope so too." I turned to look at Ace. My pulse fluttered. "I'm glad it wasn't you."

"You didn't really think I'd set the fires," he said, turning to look at me, "did you?"

"You lived there—"

Ace put the car into gear. "Where to?"

I swallowed hard. "The state park. We're having a picnic."

He backed the car down the drive. Several miles of silence later, he turned onto the road that leads into the state park. Ace glanced over at me. "There wasn't a lot of happiness in that house when I lived there."

Why on earth had I brought this up? It had nothing to do with my reason for feeding him lunch.

All of the parking spots were empty.

Ace pulled into the first slot and cut the engine. "Are we having lunch to talk about my childhood?"

"No."

"Good." He got out, came around, and opened my door. I handed him the cooler.

We sat across from each other at one of the picnic tables. A pair of mourning doves waddled along the ground searching for tasty morsels the way Bowser did in the kitchen.

I took the thermos and two plastic cups out of their bag, then filled the cups and handed one to Ace. I opened the cooler and placed one of the wrapped sandwiches in front of him.

Ace folded back the wrapping, but he didn't pick the sandwich up. Instead he stretched his arms out on the table, popped his tongue against the roof of his mouth, and rolled his lips together.

I took a bite of my sandwich.

"The truth is, Honey, I have no memory of my mother and father ever having a civil conversation. By the end of their marriage, the only communication between them consisted of shouted insults."

"I'm sorry. I didn't mean to . . ." I took a sip of tea.

Ace held up his hand, facing his palm toward me in the universal Stop sign. "It's okay, I don't like talking about my childhood, but I don't deny the facts of it either."

"Do you have brothers or sisters?"

"Nope. No siblings to commiserate with. Miss Crandell and Hattie were my salvation. They gave me a quiet place to retreat to."

"And then you moved to Chicago."

"Right. My mother met someone else, filed for divorce, remarried, and we moved. Six months later, my dad sold our place here and took a job in Saudi Arabia."

"So you had a stepdad."

"Yup. He and my mother didn't fight. My mother seemed happy. But I missed my dad, and I missed this place."

"So you weren't happy there either."

"He's a nice guy. We get along. But I hated Chicago. We lived in a high-rise in the city near the lake. I used to sit by the water and try to imagine it was the ocean. It never worked." Ace laughed and took a big bite of his sandwich.

"So you came back."

"Yup."

My heart felt like it was being struck by lightning bolts. I fought back against the strong urge to reach out and touch his hand. I kept my own hands busy tearing tiny pieces off my sandwich wrapping.

"Thanks for sharing," I said. "I'm an only child too. My parents didn't get along either. It can be lonely."

Ace pondered this for a second, nodded, and then changed the subject. "So tell me about Marie. Is she going to be okay?"

"I think so. She doesn't seem as distraught as I thought she'd be. She even admitted Jeff lacks the courage to displease his mother."

Ace pursed his lips and nodded. "So what's your childhood story?"

"Similar to yours."

This conversation was going in the wrong direction. "I disappointed my parents. My dad always talks about his friends' children who are doctors or lawyers or earned a PhD. My mother raves about the daughter of a friend who's a news anchor on a national network. My choosing to teach elementary school left them with nothing to boast about." I managed a smile. "But I love my job. It's the only job I ever wanted."

"Doing what makes you happy is important, Honey. If we do things only to please others, we open ourselves up to real trouble."

Ace had more insight into what makes one happy than I would have thought.

He finished his sandwich and crumpled the wrapping up into a ball. I should have brought dessert. I refilled his cup with tea and steeled myself to say what I'd brought him here to say before he got up to leave.

By focusing on his forehead, I managed to keep my gaze zoned in on his face. "Why did you get so upset over Miss Crandell asking me to pass on her message to you?"

Ace shrugged. "She and Hattie always have something in mind. Most of the time knowing they care about me makes me happy, but sometimes it comes close to meddling."

"They are bossy sometimes."

Ace smiled. "As sweet, loving Hattie would say, they sho' nuff is."

I laughed Della's sparkling laugh that always makes other people laugh.

Ace smiled.

I returned my gaze back to the center of his forehead. "Why did you get upset when I said with Marie staying you didn't need to help me anymore?"

Ace looked up into the tree branches overhead. "I've been helping Della for so long the place is like a second home."

I sensed Ace was having trouble adjusting to Della and Harry being gone.

I relented. If he was so attached to the place, I didn't have the heart to ban him from the premises.

"Come by whenever you want to, but I'm running the B and B on my own. Before Marie showed up, I planned to hire someone to help with breakfast and the proper trade people to do repairs."

Ace considered this for a couple of seconds. I didn't avert my gaze.

"Some of the deck boards are in bad shape," he said. "You should get them replaced soon. I can do it tomorrow if you want to hire me."

I wanted to say no. Tell him I'd hire someone else. But I couldn't. "Bowser would love helping you," I said instead. "He was in despair today because he knew you were there and he didn't see you."

Ace looked at me with a penetrating, soul-searching look that made me squirm.

"And what has caused his mistress despair?"

Good grief. I thought I'd been keeping a joyful expression on my face and the conversation serious but my tone of voice mellow. I had to be honest with Ace and with myself.

"I started thinking you showed up every morning because you thought I'd ruin the B and B's rating."

Ace looked at me and nodded. "The mornings can get hectic. I was worried about how you'd do on your own."

I wanted to sputter, mention Della had faith in me, and be indignant over his lack of faith in me, but I'd brought it up, and Ace had given me an honest answer.

I made a turn in the conversation.

"I'm going to ask Millie to live in and run the place on weekdays when school's in session. If she doesn't want the job, I'll hire someone else. I'll keep Polly on part time."

"Good. Then I'll have more time to spend with the goats." His eyes sparkled. He swung his legs over the bench seat of the picnic table.

If I'd touched any of Ace's sore spots, he'd handled it well. It was good to learn he wasn't in denial about the reality of his life or about what made him happy.

And I was pleased with myself. I might not have been quite as clear and direct as I could have been, but it was a big step in the right direction.

I got myself up and out from the table with a certain amount of grace and brushed off the seat of my capri pants.

"What I really want you to understand, Ace, is I'm freeing you from whatever obligation you feel to Della to make sure I don't ruin the business. And I'm asking you to set me free me to succeed or fail on my own."

"It's a deal," he said. "So with Marie around to help and her wedding canceled, can we dance?"

Ace was good at changing a conversation too.

"If you finish the deck tomorrow, we can practice in the afternoon."

He grinned. "Great. And, Honey, from now on I'd appreciate it if instead of telling me to show up for lunch, you'd ask me. I could have a date or something."

Our mutual laughter blended into a harmonious tune.

Except in his case, he might really have a date.

I could wish on a star to make it hard for me to like Ace, but I didn't want to. And the one thing I really should ask him, I didn't want to do either. If he and Emily were paired up, I wasn't ready yet to handle my disappointment.

Marie was in the kitchen making chocolate-chip cookies. The kitchen was filled with the scent of the pot roast she had cooking in the Crock-Pot for our dinner. The table in the kitchen was set and a vase filled with flowers from the yard sat in the center.

"So, how did lunch go?" Marie asked the minute she saw me.

I took a glass from the cupboard. "Fine. I think Ace and I have a better understanding of each other's boundaries now."

"That's always good."

"I told him I could practice tomorrow afternoon. But if my being gone isn't convenient for you, I'll cancel."

"It's fine. Will any guests be checking in while you're away?"

"No. But if someone calls and wants a room, the Sunrise Room is available Monday through Wednesday. Two double beds. The prices are on a card by the phone. You can offer a ten percent discount or fifteen if they have a military ID card."

"Okay. I can paint while you're at practice. The light on the center porch is good, and I can hear the office phone from there."

"Check in with Seeley Mayer at the co-op and show her your work."

"I might. I've got a pretty big inventory and I'm running out of storage space. It'd be great if I could sell some of them."

Chapter Eleven

Marie and I stayed busy the rest of the day. As always since we'd become friends, being together boosted our spirits. She was going to show me how to work with yeast so I could tackle the pecan rolls on my own.

Ace came by early the next morning and started on the deck boards. I let Bowser out to join him, but I didn't invite Ace in. In the afternoon, Ace and I had a good practice session. We just danced. Our thoughts and emotions about anything else, we kept to ourselves.

A week later, Ace hadn't been by and he hadn't called me to set up the next practice session. Marie had reseated the fixtures in two of the guest bathrooms and planted herbs in pots on the deck to use for omelets and for making her own sausage.

Two weeks later, Jeff called Marie and said he wanted to see her. She agreed and drove off, saying she'd be back by nightfall.

I spent the entire time she was gone in a state of sheer panic. Marie had accepted Jeff's lame excuses for why he was late or why he hadn't called in weeks for so long, I didn't trust her not to cave in again. And, most of all, I didn't trust Jeff.

At twilight, I was sitting on the porch with Bowser, willing Marie to return. When her car turned onto the drive, I uncrossed my fingers, sent up a prayer, and went down the steps.

Hurrying around to the driver's-side door, I got there at the same moment Marie stepped out. I did a quick scan of her face. She looked dismal. I gave her a hug, and then took her arm as we walked back to the porch.

Bowser greeted Marie with his usual exuberance. She stooped down to pet him. I was dying to know what had happened, but I didn't ask. Whatever was going on between Marie and Jeff wasn't my business—until Marie wanted to share.

"I need food," Marie said.

"Scrambled eggs okay?"

"Sure."

We headed for the kitchen. I got eggs and butter from the refrigerator. Marie started a fresh pot of coffee.

She ate, and then we took our coffee refills out to the deck. A full moon hung low in the sky. The air was soft. The gentle sound of waves lapping the beach added a rhythmic calm to the night. It was so soothing it wasn't possible to stay tensed up and on edge. I relaxed my body into the lounge chair.

"He wanted the ring back."

Her voice was so low, I almost missed the fact she'd spoken. I turned to look at her. She looked straight ahead.

"Did you give it back?"

"Yes. Regardless of what he paid for it, it was worthless."

Right. I wouldn't expect Marie to put up a fight over the ring. And I was glad Jeff had asked for it back—one less item to remind her of the louse.

"Choose a star and make a wish," I said. "I'll choose one too.

I think you and I have both tossed out some stuff that needed tossing out and may have turned a corner."

"What did you toss out?" she asked with a curious lilt in her voice.

Not Ace. It wasn't possible to toss out something I'd never had. "Fear. I had an epiphany a while back about all the unsuitable men I'd dated before I started my sabbatical."

"You were afraid of unsuitable men?"

"I realized I'd avoided men I thought I might like because I feared getting hurt again."

Marie turned her head to look at me. "Really?"

"Really."

"So that's why you tossed Ace out of here."

I ran my finger around the rim of my coffee cup and stared into the dark center. "I asked Ace not to come around to help in the mornings because I want to see if I can run it on my own. When he said the B and B was like a second home to him, I told him he was welcome to come around whenever he wanted to. But the problem with Ace being here is he's pushy, intrusive, and determined to get his way. And I have a hard time saying no."

So maybe this wasn't 100 percent of the truth, but it was the best I could do at the moment.

"I don't suppose you could end your sabbatical early, skip a few months."

"No." I knew I hadn't fooled Marie. And I wasn't fooling myself. But my old defenses hadn't been completely destroyed yet. "The thing is, if I draw Do Not Pass lines, Ace respects them."

"And you want him not to."

"I thought if the last kiss he gave me had been for real, he'd cross the lines, or at least try. He hasn't. I think he and Emily are together."

"I don't know, Honey. I think he shows how he feels about you by respecting your wishes and by trying to help without being asked."

"I think he was helping me because he thinks I'm not capable of running a business on my own. He even said he was worried."

"I think you've got more stuff you need to toss out." Marie yawned. "I'm off to bed. It's been a long day. But you know what?"

"What?" I got out of the lounge chair and walked to the deck rail. It was evident my fear over having my heart broken again wasn't gone.

"For years, I waited for Jeff to give me an engagement ring. Giving it back has made me feel a hundred times lighter."

" 'Night, Marie. See you in the morning."

I heard the slider open. I stayed at the rail and stared into the night. All the obstacles blocking my having a healthy relationship with a man were still in the process of being conquered. But I was making progress and, when my sabbatical officially ended, I'd redouble my efforts to find places where decent single men could be found. I'd be open to dating every man I thought would be a good candidate for falling in love with.

The next morning I was stirring up the batter for the coffee cake when Emily came through the kitchen door.

Her blond hair sparkled. She was wearing shorts that didn't cover much. She had great legs and they were a golden tan.

"Hi, Honey."

"Hey, Emily. Nice to see you." I introduced Marie and Emily.

Emily vibrated good health and goodwill. "I stopped to ask about your supply of our soap," she said.

"I think we're fine. I've been forgetting to mention it to the guests."

"Since you're running the B and B now, do you want to continue selling our soap?"

I offered Emily coffee. She accepted.

When she took the cup from me, a diamond, bigger than Marie's had been, caught the light.

"What a beautiful engagement ring," I said.

She held her hand up to give me a better view. "Thanks. I've known him for years. I thought he'd never get around to asking me to marry him."

Who? I wanted to ask. But if it was Ace, I didn't want to know. Not yet. In a day or two, I'd have had time to digest the idea, reinforce the guard around my heart, and then I could ask. I bit my lip, blinked, took a deep breath, and answered her question about the soap.

"We really don't sell enough to make it worth the bookkeeping involved. If anyone asks, I could send them to Organics if they'd want to carry it."

Emily nodded. "I was thinking of not making soap anymore. I could sell a lot more cheese. But I haven't decided how big an operation is worth the extra work. If I expand much more, I'd have to hire more people."

"More headaches," I said.

"With the two part-time workers I have now, I can handle the farm and the cheese making. And Ace will be around to fill in whenever I need an extra hand."

If it were possible for jealousy to turn a person's skin green, I'd be the same color as a frog right now.

I went back to my coffee cake, mixing the ingredients for the streusel topping. Emily and Marie began a discussion about goats. I tuned them out as best I could.

The next thing I did hear made me wish the floor would drop out from under me and the tide would take me far away from here.

Emily had said Ace was going to teach her to shag dance.

My eyes sprang a leak. There was no longer any question about my buying this place. I'd let Della know I'd keep the business open and running until the normal November closing date, but I wasn't going to buy it. She could put it on the market.

Emily called good-bye. I managed a good-bye that sounded normal to my ears and then kept busy until the guests were fed and the kitchen cleaned.

Marie put the last of the pans into the cupboard.

"I'm taking Bowser for a walk, and then I'm going to the grocery store," I said.

"Want me to come along?"

"Thanks, but I'm planning to go fast. I'll let Bowser run for a while and then I'll do a quick dash through the grocery aisles. I don't want to get caught up in any long conversations today."

"Okay. I'm going to bike around the island. I need the exercise."

Polly came back into the kitchen to tell me she was running short of the cleaner we used for the bathroom showers. I said I'd buy a case while I was at the store today.

Marie folded the dish towel she'd been using. "You okay, Honey? Your breathing doesn't sound right."

"I'm pretty sure I'm allergic to goat dander. Now that Emily has gone I'll be fine."

Marie rolled her eyes. "Right."

I left the kitchen without defending myself further. How could I, anyway? After all the years of being my best friend, Marie had a direct line to my feelings.

Maybe jealousy would be the biggest obstacle for me to get around on my way to the real thing—a love shared between two people that didn't ask more from one than from the other.

Think positive, Honey. There are multitudes of stars to wish on. You don't have to rely on only one.

Bowser jumped off the bed when I walked into our room. When he saw me pick up his leash, he started dancing in whirls. When I bent down to hook it to his collar, he licked my face. I laughed and gave him a good snuggle.

On the beach, I headed for the packed sand near the water and started to jog. Bowser kept up and didn't leave my side. I felt guilty. Now that I had more work to do, he was stuck inside the B and B most of the time and wasn't getting enough exercise. He'd be happy if he knew I wouldn't keep him here a minute longer than necessary. The fenced backyard at home allowed him the freedom to roam at will and without supervision.

I didn't go far before I was breathing in gasps. I slowed to a walk. I didn't get enough exercise either. As soon as I was home for good, I'd join a gym, get in shape. Men frequent gyms. Maybe I'd take up running marathons. Men run marathons. Getting more exercise could be a good thing in more ways than one.

By the time I got back to the B and B and stashed Bowser back in our room, the effect of the goat dander had diminished. All's fair in love and war, I reminded myself. And in every competition there's a winner. This time the winner may be Emily. Next time it could be me.

I managed a laugh. If before she left, Della had been trying to act as a matchmaker between me and Ace, hiring Emily to run the goat farm may have been a huge miscalculation on her part. Emily was goat-savvy, she was stunning to look at, she was smart, and Ace believed Emily could run a business without needing his help.

I bought the cleaning supplies and went to the grocery store on the island. I got back to the B and B in record time, put everything away, and then took out one of the bikes we keep for the guests. I'd get in some exercise and see if I could find Marie at the same time.

But it wasn't Marie whose path I crossed first as I rode along the edge of the road toward the main tourist area with its concentration of motels, restaurants, bars, and gift shops. Ace beeped his car horn and waved as he passed me headed in the opposite direction.

Nice. I didn't look back to see if he turned onto the drive of the B and B. If he did, he wouldn't find anyone there unless a guest was hanging around in the public areas—or unless he had the nerve to go up the stairs to the private quarters to find Bowser.

My instinct was to turn around and protect my territory. Ace's imaginary Resistance Corps didn't give him the right to call up Bowser to duty without my say-so. I stopped the bike.

You're hoping if you do go back, he'll be there. What would you do if he were? I started pedaling again. Marie might be at the harbor. It wasn't far.

I found her there, sitting on a bench facing the water and reading a book. I wheeled up next to the bench. "Want company?"

She looked up, closing the cover of the book she'd been reading. "Hey, Honey. Sure."

Her bike leaned against the back of the bench. I settled mine against hers and sat on the bench.

"Get your errands done?" Marie asked.

"Yup. Want to go to Siler's for dinner tonight?" I asked.

"Sure. I've been longing for another bowl of their crab soup."

We sat there—long enough for Ace to be gone from the B and B if he'd stopped—commenting on the activity around us.

We biked back.

Bowser was in our room. Nothing looked disturbed.

Marie and I got cleaned up and drove to Siler's.

Halfway through our entrée, I looked up and saw Emily in front of the hostess station. She was with a man I'd never seen before. He looked enough like her to be her brother—tall, well-built, sun-streaked blond hair.

I caught her eye and waved. She waved back but didn't come over. They were seated at a table across the room.

I gave an occasional glance their way. They were carrying on an intense conversation, but not displaying the body language one would expect during a conversation between a newly engaged couple.

Over dessert, I told Marie I wouldn't be buying the B and B.

"Why not? You're doing a great job. The guests seem happy."

"Teaching and running the B and B would take all my time. I'm thinking I may save my money and go to France next summer."

Which was true.

Marie spooned up the last of her soup. "I wonder if they make crab soup this good in France."

Sometimes I wished Marie didn't know me so well.

A week later, the mail included a short note from Della. She and Harry had gotten married in the Bahamas and were having a grand time. They'd had two charters, which were easy and fun. She'd never been happier. Her news made me happy and sad at the same time.

I went into the office to respond. I didn't want to have a phone conversation with Della—she'd ask questions—and I didn't have an e-mail address for her. I handwrote a note, wishing her the best and congratulating Harry. I told her I wouldn't be buying the B and B, and asked for instructions.

* * *

The next afternoon, Marie, Bowser, and I went to visit Miss Crandell and Hattie. The temperature was in the nineties and there was no breeze. Hattie answered the door and invited us inside where it was air-conditioned.

I deposited Bowser into Miss Crandell's outstretched arms.

"I do declare, Miss Honey, you two young ladies are prettier than any flowers in bloom," Hattie said.

Miss Crandell stroked Bowser's back. "Sit down. Sit down," she said. "I have news about Ace."

At the mention of Ace's name, Bowser perked up.

Miss Crandell gave me a sly look and a secretive smile.

Now what? "I haven't seen Ace or talked to him for a while," I said.

Miss Crandell didn't comment on my remark. Instead she started in on the story she intended to tell. "I had one sibling, a sister," she said. "She married a mainlander and moved off island. Being so far from the ocean wasn't good for her health. She was only sixty-one when she passed on. But she had a daughter, Stella. I changed my will to leave all my property to Stella. And then, three weeks ago, I learned Stella had joined her mother."

She closed her eyes for a second. Her lips moved as though offering up a silent prayer. She opened her eyes and continued. "Once I'm gone, Hattie plans on moving back to her home island, where she has family."

Hattie, sitting in a chair next to Miss Crandell, bobbed her head up and down. "That's where I plan to go."

I couldn't think what Ace had to do with all of this. But since he was the person Miss Crandell said she had news about, I imagined his part would come up at some point.

She ran her hand down the length of Bowser's back. "So, after a lot of thought, I called Ace. He's a lawyer, you know?"

I nodded my head up and down.

"He is?" Marie squeaked.

Miss Crandell ignored Marie's exclamation.

"He drew up my original will. I said I had a few changes to make. He agreed to come to the house. Hattie made potato salad. When he showed up, we insisted on his having lunch before settling down to the business of my will."

"I'm sure he enjoyed it," I said.

Miss Crandell giggled. "I'm leaving this house and the extra lot to Ace." Her countenance was glowing, her posture erect. The grin on her face and the twinkle in her eyes made her appear twenty years younger. I was stunned, but not really surprised. Her love for Ace was evident. He might have been her preferred choice in her first will, but family ranking in these parts is big, and leaving things of value to someone who wasn't next in line was rare.

"Did he get antsy and upset like he did when you and Hattie got him here on his birthday?"

"He sho' did," Hattie said, beaming one of her grins. "But I clamped my hand on his wrist, hard, and told him he was to mind his manners. When somebody does something nice for you, you thank them." Hattie's face glowed.

I burst out laughing.

Marie giggled.

Miss Crandell joined in with a few ladylike titters and then went on with her story. "After Ace settled down, we got a codicil drawn up. Hattie got Mr. Rogers from next door to come over and be the second witness."

"I'm happy for Ace. He'll love having his own place fronting the ocean," I said and then gathered up Bowser from Miss Crandell's lap.

And I was happy for Ace. I didn't know the first thing about what he might wish for except being a winner in the shag-dance world and not being tied down to work he didn't like. But I don't know anyone who wouldn't wish for a place on the first row in a beach community.

Marie was stunned. "Ace is one lucky guy," she said, as we walked back to the B and B. "How come you never told me he's a lawyer?"

"I don't think Ace works at his law practice much. He'd rather shag dance."

Which I was pretty sure was true.

Back at the B and B, Marie and I changed into bikinis and went out on the deck.

With Della gone, I hadn't had much time to work on my tan. My legs and arms still had their winter pallor.

Marie and I reclined on the lounge chairs. Bowser sprawled beneath the shade of the roof overhang.

The heat of the sun felt good.

An occasional caw of a gull or the distant shout of someone on the beach filtered up to the deck, but the salt air muted the sounds.

I drifted into a light sleep.

Bowser barked.

I sat up. Bowser was standing on his back feet with his front feet straddling the deck's railing.

"Bowser, hush." He ignored me and barked again.

"Bowser, my man." The familiar voice sent a chill down my spine. I was wearing a bikini. I hadn't brought a cover-up out here. And Ace would be in viewing range before I could get inside. I crossed my legs and then crossed my arms over my chest. It was the best I could do.

Marie sat up. "What's Bowser barking at?"

"Ace."

Ace had reached the deck gate. "Oh, hi. Sorry, I didn't know you were out here," he said. "I heard Bowser and came up to inform him the men of the Resistance are on home leave until further notice." Ace leaned on the gate. His sunglasses hid his eyes from view.

Marie giggled.

I broke out in goose bumps.

"Hey, Ace." I tried to sound neutral, giving him no clue to my true feelings about his invasion of my privacy or of the thrill I experienced seeing him again.

"Since I'm up here, can I come in for a minute?"

Before I could say no, Marie had opened the gate.

Ace sat down on one of the chairs around the table. "I'll get a pitcher of tea," Marie said.

Ace stretched out his legs. Bowser jumped into his lap. A two-year-old had a bigger vocabulary than I was capable of at the moment. Random thoughts swirled around in my mind, making no connections.

"So, how's it going, Honey?" Ace asked.

"Della and Harry got married. I wrote her and told her to put the B and B on the market."

"I know. Harry called me. I'm thinking of buying the place."

As a wedding present for Emily, I supposed. "Good. The sooner someone buys it, the better. Bowser and I need to get home."

"There's a competition in Bankston on Saturday. Betty and Sam will be there. You want to go?"

The bottom of my feet tingled with desire. Competing against Betty and Sam one more time would be fun. Soon I'd be leaving here forever. Once I was gone, Ace would be out of sight and out of mind. And I'd be out of a shag dance partner.

"Sure, Ace. It'd be fun to compete against them again."

Ace declined Marie's offer of a glass of tea. He set Bowser down.

My heart was in freefall. The thought of never seeing Ace

once I'd gone home made me sad. I knew I should enjoy each moment for what it was. *Wasting energy over what isn't, dishonors the legacy of joyful optimism left to you by your grandmother.*

Right.

"If you're buying this place, you might want to start fixing things up," I said.

Ace laughed. "I'll pick you up on Saturday at five," he said, looking at me with something I wanted to believe was more than friendship in his eyes.

He waved good-bye and disappeared down the stairs.

Bowser stood at the closed gate looking sad.

Chapter Twelve

Two days after Ace asked for what he wanted and I'd said yes again, I got an e-mail from Della. She'd be listing the B and B with Drucker's. Cam Drucker would come by on Monday to check over the property.

I guess Ace had decided not to buy it after all.

Every inch of me sank into deep-worry mode. When the B and B sold, Della would have no more business ties here. This was the house she grew up in . . . at least the older part. She and Harry hadn't been married for long, and they hadn't been running charters for someone else for long either. Della wouldn't be without resources. She'd get a lot of money from the sale of the B and B to add to the money she got from selling the goat farm, but still . . .

I stumbled out of the office, grabbed a bike from the rack, and rode off, pedaling as if demons were chasing me—or sharks.

The harbor was quiet. The marina was half-empty. I found a bench set beneath a tree that gave me refuge from the direct sun. It looked pretty clean.

I watched a man climb aboard a sailboat and maneuver it away from the dock. The sail filled with air and the boat skimmed over the water. Sailing lessons ranked high on my list of new things to do. But they wouldn't be here.

Taking in several deep breaths calmed me down a bit. My worrying over the decisions other people made had never changed anything. And if the people I wasted so much of my time worrying about found out later that they'd made a wrong decision, except for my listening and being supportive, the consequences were theirs to deal with.

I leaned back against the bench. Tonight, I'd sit out on the deck and choose a star, and wish for a quick sale of the B and B. The sooner I got home, the sooner I could get started on the rest of my life.

Climbing back on the bike, I pedaled at a less frantic pace back to the B and B.

I found Marie in her room and gave her the news about the pending sale.

"Maybe it's for the best, Honey."

Maybe it is.

On Saturday, Ace picked me up for the competition.

As he turned the car onto Circle Road, I glanced over at him. I longed to close my eyes and let my fingers trace the contours of his face. I wrenched my eyes away and stared through the windshield. "Since we haven't practiced for a while, I hope we haven't lost our edge," I said.

"We'll do fine. Thanks for coming tonight."

He asked about Bowser and Marie. We talked about Della's decision to sell. Neither of us sounded joyful.

When we got to the place where the competition was being held, Sam and Betty greeted us at the door. They introduced us to friends of theirs, Carol Hammer and Mike Jones. Mike's company was transferring him to Iowa. He'd be leaving next week.

"It'll be tough leaving," he said. "But if I want to keep a job, I have to move."

"Change is the order of the day," I said.

Ace took my hand and gave it a squeeze.

Prickles raced up the length of my arm. The physical effect Ace had on me was beyond my control, but the mental effect could be controlled—if I tried hard. One last dance competition, a few more days on the island, and Ace would be a nice memory.

We danced in complete synchronization.

"I think we won." Ace whispered in my ear when we were announced as one of the three finalists. "You were perfection tonight."

My heart trilled from his praise and from the anticipation of our possible win. I cupped my hand around my mouth and leaned in. He smelled of Della's herb soap and something else—something male and powerful.

"You were too," I said. "But don't count out Sam and Betty."

I stepped sideways—far enough from Ace to lessen the power of his scent.

We did win, and the ride home was surreal.

Ending my dance partnership with Ace would also end my shag dancing—not because my love for him and my love of shag dancing were intertwined, but because partnering with someone less skilled than Ace would be painful.

At the B and B, Ace parked and got out of the car. "Okay if I say hello to Bowser?"

"Sure. Wait on the porch. I need to let him out."

"Hey, Honey," Marie called as I came up the stairs.

I looked into her room. She was watching television.

"How'd it go?" she asked.

"We won."

"Wow. Congratulations. So, is it over?"

"Yup. I'm taking Bowser down. Ace is on the porch waiting to say hello."

"Maybe Ace should get a dog of his own."

"Good idea. I'll pass that along."

As soon as I opened the door of the bedroom, Bowser dashed through and flew down the stairs.

I opened the porch door. Bowser went straight to Ace.

"Your lordship," Ace said. "Good to see you again."

I held on to the edge of the door to steady my knees. I wasn't very good at ending things. "I'm making coffee. You want a cup?"

"Sounds good."

Winning tonight had pumped up Ace's adrenaline, and caffeine would only add to his late-night energy. No telling when he'd leave. But I'd offered him coffee to give myself a chance to regain some self-control before thinking through the consequences.

I looked around the familiar kitchen while the coffee brewed. Someone else would be fixing the breakfasts here soon. A feeling of nostalgia washed over me. Change is the order of things, and resilient people move on. But sometimes change hurts.

I took two cups of coffee out to the porch.

Ace and I watched Bowser as he explored the yard. "You make great coffee," Ace said.

"Thanks."

The whispering sound from a light breeze and the whirring sound of the cicadas filled the silence. Tomorrow I'd find the papery outer shells from their molt attached to posts and tree trunks. Maybe, when I looked back on my time here this summer, I'd see I had shed some things I'd outgrown too.

Bowser came back up on the porch and went straight to Ace again. Ace picked him up and set him in his lap.

"Maybe you should get a dog," I said.

"Might be hard finding a dog as great as Bowser. Almost as hard as finding a perfect shag dance partner."

"There are a lot of talented shag dancers. I'm positive you'll find someone without much trouble."

"It's not so much talent as it is the ability to communicate with each other."

"Hmm." What Ace had said was true. But this time he wouldn't get his way. I wasn't going to spend my weekends driving for miles and spending my money to stay in motels so he could have a dance partner. I'd rather save up for a trip to Europe, and for sailing lessons, and for taking advantage of other new challenges that came my way. It was time to move on, like Della, before I got too old.

I drifted into a kind of hazy reality. Everything that had been making me anxious for the past few weeks had worked out. Della was married and said she was happy. The B and B would soon be someone else's to run and worry about. Ace and I seemed to have come to an unspoken agreement about our relationship, and Marie wasn't marrying Jeff and was handling it well.

There wasn't much left for me to worry over.

"You're welcome to visit Bowser whenever you want. Just call. If I won't be home, I can leave him in the backyard."

Great. Invite Ace to show up at your house to see Bowser so you might see him too and get all sorrowful again.

The rocking chair next to me creaked. Ace stood up.

I stood up.

The next thing I knew, I was in his arms and he was pulling me close. His cheek brushed mine. "Thanks, Honey, I had a great time tonight." His warm breath caressed my ear.

"I did too—" His lips found mine. What more I'd been going to say was no longer important.

The kiss lasted too long and not long enough. Ace kept his arms around me as he leaned back and stared into my eyes. Long seconds passed, and then he reached up and tweaked my nose. "Sorry, I forgot to ask," he said.

"Good-bye, Ace," I said. "I wish you and Emily and the goats all the best."

"Thanks."

Before I could wipe my cheeks dry, Ace's car was going down the drive.

I picked up the coffee cups and carried them inside.

"I don't know if you should be friends with Ace," I said to Bowser. "An honorable man who may be engaged to marry someone else shouldn't have kissed me with such passion."

And an honorable woman wouldn't have returned his kiss with such passion either.

Upstairs, the light was on in Marie's room. I tapped on the door.

"Come in," she called.

I opened the door and stuck my head in. Marie was curled up in the chair. A book lay open on her lap.

"'Night, Marie."

"Honey, can you come in for a minute?"

I stepped inside Marie's room and sat down on the window seat.

"Jeff called a few minutes ago."

"And?"

"He said he loved me, he didn't want to sell cars anymore, and he didn't care what his mother wanted."

"Wow."

"He signed a contract to teach math at a school in Texas. We're getting married at the Farmington courthouse on Friday and then leaving for Texas right after."

If a shark had taken a chunk out of my body, I couldn't have been more shocked.

"You're moving to Texas?"

"Fort Worth."

"But what about—?"

"I'm driving back to your house on Monday, resigning from my teaching job, and packing. We're renting a moving truck. Jeff has told his dad but not his mother. His dad gave us his blessing, and he told Jeff he'd handle the situation at home once we were married and on our way out of town."

I managed to get to my feet and gave Marie a big hug without toppling over. "Jeff must love you a lot."

"I think we'll be happy."

"I'll miss you. Maybe, at the end of this school year, I'll move to Texas too. I've heard there are more single men in Texas than almost anywhere." I laughed, even though I wasn't feeling very happy about Marie living so far away or about my response to Ace's kiss. " 'Night, Marie. I'll see you in the morning," I called as I went out the door.

Bowser looked up as I entered our bedroom. "It'll be me and you against the world again," I said. "Della's gone, Marie will be gone soon, and Ace will be gone too."

I curled up on the floor next to Bowser and let my heart crack into little pieces. Bowser licked my cheek and nestled close to me. A long time later, I climbed into my bed.

On Monday it rained. Marie packed her car and then helped me with breakfast. When the last pan was put away, she gave me a quick hug and then hurried out of the kitchen.

"Write," I called, as a new flood of tears spilled down my cheeks.

Polly strolled into the kitchen. Her eyes were full of compassion. "Is there anything I can do?"

"No. But thanks for asking."

I turned my back, dried my face on a dish towel, then stood by the sliding glass door looking out. On the horizon, rain merged with the ocean, creating a gray blur that matched my mood. As I stood there awash in gloom, the rain clouds moved on and the sun peeped out.

I heard the wheels of the vacuum cleaner roll across the kitchen floor.

"Polly, I'll be on the deck if you need me."

When I heard the whir of the vacuum's motor, I filled a glass with tea and took it out to the umbrella table on the deck.

I went around for Bowser and brought a towel from the bathroom to dry off a lounge chair.

Bowser stayed below the deck. I left the deck gate open for him, then moved a side table and one of the lounge chairs beneath the limited shelter of the overhang and retrieved my glass of tea. Bowser came bounding up the steps to the deck, followed by Ace. I was beginning to wonder if Ace camped beneath the deck and waited for me to come out so he could vex me.

"Hey," Ace said, sounding confident I'd be glad to see him. He smiled his dazzling smile. "I came by to tell you my news. Bowser greeted me in the front yard, and like a good scout he led me to my quarry."

I looked at Bowser. "You know you're not supposed to be in the front yard unless I'm with you."

Bowser looked puzzled.

"I think he caught my scent," Ace said, as he pulled the other lounge chair over, dried it off, and stretched out. He placed his hands behind his head. "I've been overseeing a loggerhead turtle nest. If they're on time, the hatching should be tonight. You want to keep watch with me?"

I'd never seen a turtle nest hatching before. The people I know who had, spoke about it with a strange reverence in their voice. Going with Ace to watch baby turtles emerge from their nest beneath the sand and then scurry toward the ocean shouldn't be difficult to manage. There was bound to be a crowd. And with Marie gone, it wasn't as if I had anything else to do tonight or anyone else to hang out with.

"Sure." Good grief. Once I was home and beyond temptation, I'd have to work on saying no.

Ace picked me up at dusk. Near nest number forty-three, we spread straw beach mats on top of the sand and sat down to wait.

By the time the turtle nest started to simmer, with a slow stirring of the sand over the nest, a dozen or more spectators had joined us. The first tiny black head poked out, followed by a flipper. Everyone gasped, and then the entire crowd seemed to hold its breath for a second. You could sense the excitement building. Then the sand began to boil, a more volatile shifting of the beach, as the rest of fifty or more hatchlings forced their way to the surface.

I watched in awe as the tiny turtles emerged and then went as fast as they could go toward the ocean. Several volunteers worked to keep them heading in the right direction and to protect them from predators.

When the last of the hatchlings had entered the water, the crowd dispersed. Ace and I were alone.

"Life goes on, Honey."

"And sometimes it's a miracle."

He turned to look at me. "I'm going to buy the B and B."

I wasn't surprised. One day he'd own Miss Crandell's house, which could be turned into a B and B too. But Ace would keep Della's business going, and if Della ever wanted to return, I was pretty sure he'd sell it back to her.

"You'll do a great job."

"Since you're familiar with the routine, I was wondering if you'd be willing to help out during the summer months."

"Me?"

"We could keep our shag dance partnership going."

"I can't give you an answer right now, Ace. I'm thinking about traveling during the summers."

"And, Honey—"

"What?"

"Would it be okay if I kissed you?"

I sprang up and started to roll my mat. "You shouldn't be kissing me, Ace. It isn't honorable." I glared at him.

"I don't . . . What isn't honorable? You wanted me to ask permission, and I did," he huffed.

He wouldn't get his way. Not this time. I looked out at the dark ocean.

"Emily came by the B and B the other day. She was wearing her engagement ring."

Ace looked up at the sky. "Star light, star bright . . ." He grabbed hold of my hand and then forced me to look at him. "So that's what's bothering you?"

"Your kissing me is what's bothering me."

"I hoped it would."

This time I huffed. "I'm walking back to the B and B."

"It's a mile and a half, Honey."

"After tomorrow, I'll be gone. With your turtle nest hatched, and Emily doing all the work at the goat farm, you should have plenty of time to run the B and B."

I stomped off as best I could with shifting sand underfoot. The excess moisture in my eyes got burned off by the heat of my anger.

The going got easier once I reached the edge of the pavement. I walked along at a good pace and planned out my future. I'd honor my teaching contract for the year, and then I'd put my house on the market and find a teaching job in Texas.

Maybe I'd learn to rope cattle.

The next morning, I served breakfast and chatted with the guests as if everything were normal. Most of them knew Ace. They wouldn't feel cheated to find him cooking and serving breakfast the next morning. Truth be told, they might be happy. Ace is a much better cook than I am.

I worked on the books in the office while Polly finished cleaning the guest rooms. When I told her I'd be leaving first thing the next day, and Ace would be taking over, she looked at me with one of those questioning looks people give you when they want more information but don't want to ask. I didn't explain the reason for my sudden departure. Instead I said I'd finish the laundry, and she could go for the day.

With the sheets and towels washed and dried and put away, I took Bowser to Miss Crandell's house for one last visit.

Hattie responded to my knock. She looked distraught. "Oh, Miss Honey, come in. I'm waiting on the doctor to come see to Miss Crandell. She coughed the entire night and none of my remedies helped."

I tied Bowser to the porch railing. "Wait here," I said to him. "Miss Crandell isn't feeling well today."

I followed Hattie into Miss Crandell's bedroom. She was sitting up in her bed, propped up by pillows behind her back. A vaporizer spewing Vicks fumes sat on the dresser. I told Hattie

I'd sit with Miss Crandell and she was to go lie down. I said I'd call her as soon as the doctor got here.

Hattie didn't protest. She looked exhausted.

I sat down in the chair pulled up next to Miss Crandell's bed.

"I'm glad you're here, Honey." Her voice was strained. "Ace stopped in last week. He's in love with you, you know."

"He's in love with Emily."

She covered a spell of coughing with her hand.

I sat still until the coughing stopped.

Miss Crandell looked surprised. She sat forward, tumbling the neat stack of pillows behind her back. "Why, Ace didn't say a word about Emily. All he talked about was you, and what a great dancer you are, and how the two of you won your last shag dance competition."

"He loves having won a few shag dance contests."

Her coughing started up again.

I got up, set the pillows back in place, insisted she lie back, and then I tucked the covers around her frail body.

She closed her eyes and dozed off. Her breathing was labored.

Where was the doctor, anyway? Several young women on the island were nearing the end of their pregnancies. Maybe he was delivering a baby.

I sat there for a little more than two hours.

When Miss Crandell woke, I told her about Marie. She said she was delighted Marie had taken a stand and that Jeff had come to his senses. Her voice trembled. "Love's a funny thing, Honey."

"It is," I said.

I told her Ace would be buying the B and B. She looked surprised but didn't comment. She listened while I talked about Della and Harry, and about my memories of my grandmother. I told her I'd be teaching again in the fall.

The depth of her coughs had lessened. She dozed off again. When she woke a half hour later, the color had returned to her cheeks. I filled her glass with water and offered it to her. She took a sip, then lay back and closed her eyes again.

A loud rapping sounded on the front door.

Dr. Robinson stood there with tired eyes and his black bag in his hand.

"Miss Crandell's dozing," I said, as he came inside. "She looks better and her coughs aren't as racking."

"That's good news. These two never call me until Hattie has run through all of her home remedies." Dr. Robinson laughed. "By the time they get around to asking for my help, the germs are ready to surrender."

Dr. Robinson went into Miss Crandell's bedroom.

I went to wake Hattie.

She rolled off her bed. "Providence sent you here this morning, Miss Honey. I was near collapse." She hugged me tight. "How's she doing?"

"I expect the worst may be over," I said. "She's been dozing, and her coughing has quieted some."

Hattie joined Dr. Robinson. I waited in the living room until he came out of Miss Crandell's bedroom.

"I'll be back to check on her tonight," he said. "But I think she'll be as good as new in a few days."

I saw him out and then went into the bedroom. Miss Crandell waved a frail hand through the air.

I told Hattie I'd be leaving the island and that I'd be teaching in the fall. I told her Ace was buying the B and B, and Marie was getting married after all and would be moving to Texas. She didn't look surprised by any of this.

"It's not so far you can't come for a visit and bring Bowser to see us," Miss Crandell said.

Hattie chuckled. "Miss Crandell and me's still got business left to do, Miss Honey."

An unexpected burst of optimism and joy washed over me. I had no idea why. Maybe it was because, like Marie, I'd taken a stand and had stood firm.

"I'm thinking of joining Marie in Texas at the end of the next school year. If I decide to go, I'll come for a long visit beforehand."

"Uh-huh," said Hattie. Miss Crandell's laugh turned into a fit of coughing.

"I promise," I vowed and then said good-bye and let myself out.

I untied Bowser. "Sorry, you can't go in today. Miss Crandell is better, but she's still pretty weak."

At dusk, I went out to the deck and spent the next few hours listening to the ocean and watching the stars blink. When the air grew chilly, I went inside and managed to fall asleep.

My alarm went off at five. I showered and dressed, fed Bowser, and went down to make coffee. I'd miss being here. The B and B was the kind of place that seeps into one's heart and doesn't leave. I filled a mug with coffee, took it out to the deck, and offered a silent toast to Della, my aunt, my friend, my mentor. Maybe on spring break, I'd go to Florida and visit her and Harry if they were going to be in port for a day or two.

I got a few last things into the car. With Bowser secure in his carrier, I headed home. Halfway there, I stopped for coffee and called Marie to let her know I was on my way.

She yelped her delight. "You'll be here in time to witness my wedding ceremony Friday. I wanted to ask you to come, but I knew the B and B would be full and you'd be busy."

"I no longer work there."

"Why? What happened?"

"Ace decided to buy it. He's taking over the running of the place while the sale goes through."

"Did he fire you?"

"I fired myself."

"Oh." Marie's voice had lost its energy.

"Bye, Marie. I'll talk to you when I get home." I ended the call before she could ask more questions.

Pulling into my driveway for the first time in weeks made me feel settled again. I loved my house. I loved my life here. There would be no surprises. My sabbatical from dating was back on with no waffling; I might even extend it.

The kitchen smelled like roast chicken.

I took a diet soda out of the refrigerator.

"You must have been speeding."

"Hey, Marie." She was wearing pajamas. "I'm not answering questions right now, so don't waste your time," I said.

"Okay. I'm roasting a chicken for dinner."

It seemed early to start dinner, but Marie probably had a lot to do today.

"Smells good."

"You want to go shopping later? I've tried on a lot of dresses, but I can't decide on one for my wedding."

"Sure. Have you looked at Bidels?"

"Bidels is way too expensive."

"It's your wedding, Marie. A once-in-a-lifetime event."

At least it was a one-time event for some people.

"You're right. We'll go there first and look, even if I don't buy anything."

We got to Bidels just as the owner was unlocking the door. The clothes they carry are expensive. Five years before, I'd bought a suit on sale here. Even on sale it was expensive, but the quality of the fabric was worth the price, and because it has classic lines, I still wear it.

The owner welcomed us with a big smile and a warm offer of help. Bidels customers get the same personal attention high rollers in Vegas get.

Marie explained she was getting married in a ceremony at the courthouse. She said she wanted something special that she could wear again.

Without asking her size, the owner escorted Marie to the size-six section and then took down two dresses and a suit. Marie went to try them on. The dresses were great. The suit was perfect. A fine-woven ivory fabric had been fashioned into a long-sleeved, fitted jacket and a straight skirt. Marie looked at the price tag and gulped.

"Our end-of-season sale starts tomorrow," the owner said. "Twenty percent off the ticket price."

"Will you hold it for me until tomorrow?" Marie asked.

"I'd be delighted to. I can't imagine anyone looking more beautiful wearing this suit."

When Marie emerged from the dressing room in her own clothes again, Bidels' owner took charge of the suit. "I'll be back tomorrow, early," Marie said. "Thank you for your help."

I decided the extra cost is worth it when you shop at a store with a staff who can look at you and pick out the right size, and the perfect style, and flattering colors. Once I paid off the excess charges on my credit card, I would watch for Bidels sale ads.

Marie and I left and went in search of the perfect pair of shoes.

On Friday, at ten thirty in the morning, Marie and Jeff were married. Jeff's brother and I stood as witnesses. Marie made a beautiful bride. The suit from Bidels was enhanced by her dewy-eyed look.

After the brief civil ceremony, and a series of photographs snapped by me and Jeff's brother at different scenic spots around town, we went back to my house for a celebration brunch.

An hour and fifteen minutes later, Marie and Jeff had changed out of their wedding clothes, climbed into a rental truck packed with their belongings, and started off, heading west.

Soon after, the few guests and Jeff's brother left. It was just Bowser and me again. Silence pounded my ears. Loneliness soaked into my bones. I curled up on the couch and flicked on the TV, but I didn't see or hear much of what was on. When my windows grew dark, I got up, turned off the TV, fed Bowser, and went out for a quick dinner. After eating, I stopped at the bookstore and perused the titles of books in the nonfiction section. I looked for a book on emotional survival. Several titles seemed to speak to the issue of making the best of difficult times. But I figured none of them contained better advice than being joyful and optimistic regardless of the immediate circumstances.

I wandered over to the romance fiction section. I chose a book by one of my favorite authors, bought it, and headed for home.

Bowser welcomed me back by lapping the foyer a couple of times. I let him out into the backyard. I sat on the patio and made a mental list of all the positive things that had happened this summer. I'd learned a lot about my strengths, about my readiness to risk having my heart broken, and about love.

The following day, I worked in the yard, pulling weeds out of the neglected flower beds, and then went to the library and got a couple of do-it-yourself home-repair books. I still hadn't learned how to work with yeast or tried to make Della's pecan rolls, but as soon as I mastered a few simple home repairs, yeast bread would be my next project.

On Sunday, another of the third-grade teachers called and invited me to her house for a cookout that night. I said yes. Her husband was some kind of engineer at a big plant in the next town. Maybe a single male friend of his would be at the cookout. And, even though my sabbatical was back on full strength, I was no longer running away from promising men.

I dressed in my best capri pants, a sleeveless knit top, and a pair of sandals I'd bought where Marie purchased her wedding shoes.

At the cookout, I was introduced to two single males with promise. Both of them had moved here in the previous month from the Midwest. I mentioned my love for the history of this area. Each expressed interest in visiting the historical places nearby. Given the opportunity to share, I said I'd be happy to show them around the Revolutionary War National Battlefield. The second man asked me to dinner. I accepted.

Things were looking up.

But when I told Bowser about having met not one but two interesting single men, he turned his back on me, and then he curled up in his bed without our nighttime cuddle.

Maybe he wasn't so happy about being back at home after all. When I went out, he was here alone. At the B and B there were people around during the day, and even if he was upstairs he could hear them. There was a constant arrival of new guests who gushed over him. And I think being separated from the commander of the Resistance Corps probably depressed him.

Truth be told, it depressed me too.

Chapter Thirteen

I signed up for a Tai Chi class to get myself centered and mentally prepared for the beginning of the school year.

Two weeks before the teachers were due at school, my phone rang.

It was Ace. Miss Crandell wasn't doing well; he thought I'd want to know. I thanked him and quickly tossed some of my things into a small bag and put Bowser's things in my car. Twenty minutes after the call, Bowser and I were on our way to the island.

Strands Motel allows small pets. I took a room, filled Bowser's bowls, told him to behave, and set off for Miss Crandell's.

Hattie came to the door looking sad. She gave me one of her big hugs.

"Can I see her?" I asked.

"She'll want you, Miss Honey. She goes in and out."

Hattie led the way to Miss Crandell's bedroom. Pillows elevated her head and shoulders. Her coloring was pale, her breathing shallow, her eyes closed. I took her frail hand in mine. Tears rolled down my cheeks in a silent tribute to her. "Thank you,

Miss Crandell," I murmured. "In your quiet way, you renewed my ability to weather life's storms this summer."

She opened her eyes. Her thin lips parted. The fingers of her hand tightened on mine. "Don't despair, Honey . . ." Her weakened voice trailed off and her eyes closed again.

"I promise not to, Miss Crandell." I laid her hand back atop the covers and turned to see Hattie swiping at her cheeks. "I'll be at Strands for the next few days. If there's any change or anything I can do, call me."

"I sho' will, Miss Honey. Miss Crandell is on her way home. It won't be long."

"I'll let myself out, Hattie." I walked out to the porch.

Ace stood at the bottom of the steps, leaning against the handrail. He looked up at me and held out his hand. I walked down the steps and grabbed hold.

We went around to the beach side. Neither of us spoke as we strolled in the direction of the B and B.

When we were in front of it, he stopped me. "I made a fresh pitcher of sweet tea, hoping you might come in."

Words of dissent stuck in my throat. This time I needed to let Ace get his way. I started up the sand toward the B and B with Ace close beside me. We climbed the steps to the deck, in silence.

"Have a seat. I'll be right back," Ace said, his voice full of sadness.

A flood of feelings threatened to swamp my ability to keep control of my emotions. With Della gone, Miss Crandell was my last personal link to this magical place. After she was gone, I'd have no reason to come here. My finger caught the first tear.

Ace handed me a paper napkin and a glass of tea. The tips of his fingers touched mine as I took them from him. My hand trembled as I blotted my cheeks dry. I took a long sip and drew in a deep breath of the fresh ocean air.

I managed a tiny smile.

"Are you enjoying being in charge of the B and B full time?" I asked.

Ace leaned back in his chair. There was no cockiness in his expression or in his body language. "I always thought being an innkeeper was my true calling, and I was right. I'm thinking of offering dinner during the main tourist season."

"If the food's great, it might work."

"I'm closing my law practice."

This didn't surprise me much. I'd figured practicing law was at the bottom of Ace's list of the things he was passionate about.

"How are Emily and the goats?"

"She's doing a super job at the farm and is making plans for the wedding."

"The two of you make a great pair. I wish you happiness." The cracked pieces of my heart were cracking into even smaller pieces.

Ace gave me the strangest look I'd ever seen on anyone's face. "You think Emily is marrying me? Is that why, when I asked to kiss you, you said no and got so angry? I thought it was because you thought I was taking advantage of the moment."

I knocked over my glass of tea. The cold liquid pooling on my leg let me focus on something other than what he'd just said.

I stood up to avoid the puddle of tea about to start running over the edge of the table.

Ace got up too. "Your favorite defensive move, Honey."

"What?"

"Knocking something over."

"Well, I—" My giggles interfered with my desire to deny the obvious. The next thing I focused on was how right it felt to have Ace's arms around me. He pressed a finger across my lips so I couldn't speak. "So all this time you thought I was in love with Emily. Why didn't you ask me?"

I tried to move my lips to answer. He pressed harder.

"Is that why you left before the summer was over?" I could only blink my eyes in response.

He lifted his finger from my lips. "Honey, I—"

"I didn't ask because, if you said you were, it would have broken my heart."

"But you thought Emily and I were engaged anyway."

"Until I knew for sure, there was always the possibility I was wrong."

His arms tightened around me, and this time it was his lips pressed on mine preventing me from saying anything.

I pressed back. No words could have been more honest or as clear.

The beach sounds disappeared, and my sense of time and space no longer existed. Only the two of us mattered

Ace broke off the kiss. But he didn't let me go. His cheek rested against mine. His breath warmed my ear.

I couldn't keep the joy I was feeling silent. A tiny sob of relief and of happiness escaped.

"It's okay, Honey," Ace whispered in my ear. "Will you stay awhile?"

I stepped back, gazing deep into his beautiful eyes. "Yes."

"Wait here. I'll be back in seconds."

I looked up at the sky to find a star. But instead of a wish, I gave thanks for Hattie and Miss Crandell and for my grandmother and Della.

When Ace returned, he had a blanket, a thermos, and plastic cups.

Sitting next to each other in the shelter of the dunes, with the moonlight creating a golden path across the water, Ace and

I talked through the issues we each had about love and commitment and marriage. We named our emotions. We drank the cold tea and then warmed our lips with kisses.

Leaving the blanket and tea things on the beach, Ace walked me back to Strands. The minute he saw Ace, Bowser started doing whirls around Strands' walkway. Ace scooped him up. "Your lordship, I'm delighted to see you're back safe. I feared I'd lost my best trooper."

I laughed. "Do you have others?"

Ace narrowed his eyes and skewed his lips. "Sorry, but the number of members is classified information."

"What does the Resistance Corps defend against, anyway?" I asked.

"Wily females." Ace burst out laughing. "Our defense methods have not been perfected yet."

He kissed me good night.

Before I went inside, I chose another star, and this time I made a wish, and said a prayer for Miss Crandell.

The next day Miss Crandell went home. I pictured my grandmother with a joyous countenance greeting her old friend.

Hattie had told Ace she didn't feel right staying at the house with Miss Crandell gone. He'd helped her pack a few things and put her in my old room at the B and B. He offered her a job as his assistant cook. She declined.

Two days later, I sat beside Ace and Hattie in the small island church during Miss Crandell's memorial service. At the cemetery, the three of us stood close together, drawing strength from one another.

In the afternoon, Hattie's great-niece would be here to pick her up and drive her to her home island, where she'd spend the remainder of her life surrounded by members of her family.

Ace went to fix lunch. Hattie motioned me into her room.

She sat in the chair. "Sit on the bed, Miss Honey. I have some things I have to say."

I sat. "I'm so—"

She raised her hand. "No need for sorrow, Miss Honey," she said and then blotted her eyes. "Miss Crandell and I had a good run. Better than most gets."

I nodded my agreement. "Mr. Ace is a good man, Miss Honey. Miss Crandell's last wish was the two of you would overcome your fears."

"We have," I said. "Or at least we're trying hard."

Hattie grinned. "By the way the two of you've been looking at each other, I figured a lot of things had gotten straightened out."

"I'm sorry we weren't in time to let Miss Crandell know."

"I do believe she knows."

I started to stand to give Hattie a hug and then go see if I could help Ace.

"Sit down, Miss Honey. I ain't finished yet."

I plopped back down.

She waited until I'd settled and she had my full attention.

"Dress the boiled potatoes with a little vinegar and sugar before they go cold." Hattie chuckled and pushed herself to her feet. She held out her arms to me. "You let me know the day, and I'll get myself back here for the wedding. I promised Miss Crandell we'd be there."

"So, Miss Crandell was positive Ace and I would work things out."

Hattie laughed her deep, resonant laugh. "From the minute she laid eyes on the two of you together, she knew."

Arm in arm, Hattie and I headed to the kitchen. Ace looked up from the stove. "I suppose the two of you have been conspiring."

Hattie laughed. "That we have, Mr. Ace."

Ace served us chicken salad with grapes and walnuts mixed

in and hot biscuits. Hattie raved as she took a second helping of salad. As we ate, Hattie and Ace shared stories from years ago. I listened and laughed and let the warm glow surrounding me fuse the loose pieces of my heart together.

Hattie's great-niece showed up on schedule. We packed Hattie's things into the car. Ace helped Hattie into the passenger seat. Hattie sniffed. My eyes filled with tears. I looked at Ace. A single tear trickled down his cheek.

As they drove off, Ace put his arm around my shoulders and pulled me close. "Hattie and Miss Crandell always got their way, Honey." He laughed, turned me toward him, and then without asking, he kissed me for a long time while the mockingbird in a nearby tree serenaded us with a medley of other birds' songs.

Ace ended the long kiss with a series of sweet little kisses and then walked with me toward the porch.

"I'm glad they didn't fail this time," I said, somewhat breathless.

"Hello, you two." The voice came from behind us. Sam and Betty were coming up the drive on bikes. We invited them inside, showed them around, and then settled on the porch. They told us about the competitions Ace and I had missed and shared their news about having qualified for Nationals.

We weren't surprised.

We told them our news.

They weren't surprised.

We promised we'd be at Nationals to support them. And that we'd be competing against them again next year.

After they left, Ace and I sat on the porch holding hands and working out the details of our future as the ocean wrapped its enchantment around us.

"I want to fulfill my contract for the school year," I said.

"Mr. Delaney would have a hard time trying to replace two of his third-grade teachers both leaving at this late date."

"We'll do what you planned on doing when you were determined to keep the place open so Della could come back if she got fed up with Harry. But instead of Millie running it on weekdays, I'll be here."

When school was in session, I'd be driving down with Bowser each Friday and leave on Sunday night. Ace would move into Miss Crandell's house, which now belonged to him, and start renovating it while he ran the B and B.

Before we were married, I'd stay at the B and B when I was on the island. Where Bowser slept on those weekends would be up to Bowser.

Ace and I walked arm in arm back to Strands.

"I'll come help you in the morning with breakfast and then I'll have to leave. School starts in two weeks. Teachers have to report a week ahead of time, and I have a lot to do."

"It'll be lonely here without you, Honey."

"I'll call every night, and I'll be back on Friday."

I agreed on Bowser spending the night with Ace.

Ace gave me a quick kiss.

Even this brief physical contact elicited tingles that were becoming difficult to corral. I said good night, stepped into my room, and quickly closed the door.

It was well past dawn when I woke.

I dressed in a hurry and jogged to the B and B.

My first glimpse of Ace made me smile. This gorgeous man who could cook for himself, who loved animals—both farm and domestic—and who could shag dance better than anyone I'd ever danced with was going to marry me. My entire being was flooded with joy and optimism.

When the breakfast things were cleared away, Bowser and I

headed for home. As soon as I had let Bowser out into the backyard, I called Della to let her know the sad news and the happy news. And then I called Marie to tell her.

"I tried to tell you," she said, sounding smug.

This year spring break was a real break, unlike the cruise last year. On the first Saturday, Ace and I were married in the small island church. Fresh from the groomer and with a turquoise bow attached to his collar, Bowser sat on the front pew along with Hattie, who was wearing a pink chiffon dress and matching hat. Sitting between them was a framed photograph of Miss Crandell.

Marie stood up with me. Harry stood up with Ace. Della catered the wedding brunch—which included Hattie's contribution, a giant bowl of her potato salad.

Sam and Betty came. Emily and her fiancé were there, along with several of the island residents who'd been friends of my family and who had known Ace for years. His mother and stepfather came from Chicago, and my father and his wife came from California. Even my mother managed to get to my wedding. Ace's father sent his regrets and wished us well.

When all the guests had left, Ace and I and Hattie and Bowser went to Miss Crandell's grave and placed my wedding flowers there in remembrance of the woman who'd loved all of us, who'd taught Ace and me important lessons about life, and who'd conspired with Hattie to make this day possible.

That night, as I lay beside Ace, listening to him breathe, I sighed with contentment.

The right man had showed up at the right time.

For our twenty-fifth wedding anniversary, I'd send an announcement to our local newspaper along with a photo of the two of us smiling.

Ace turned over. My fingers drifted over the contours of his face. And then, without asking permission, he kissed me.

Made in the USA
Charleston, SC
30 November 2012